ALL I'LL EVER NEED

J.P.BOWIE

ALL I'LL EVER NEED

Dedication

As always, my thanks to Claire and Nicki, the
wonderfully supportive owners of Totally Bound, and
to my super helpful editor Sue, and all the other
people at TB who are such a pleasure to work with.
And this year I can say thanks to my husband Phil for
being in my life and bringing me joy and inspiration.
We were legally married in May 2014.

Chapter One

Edward Conway couldn't remember just how long he'd been standing on the opposite side of the street from the Rockin' Bar's entrance, but he was sure of one thing—his feet, hands and nose were way too cold, and if he didn't grow a pair and get his ass inside, he'd most likely come down with some kind of flu-related ailment. It was an unseasonably chilly night in southern California, one he'd been unprepared for, venturing out earlier without his bomber jacket that would have shielded him from the bitter wind.

"God, but you're a pussy," he muttered. What could be so terrible? It was a gay bar—a place he'd wanted to visit ever since he'd arrived in LA, just to see what it was like. Maybe he'd meet someone nice, talk, share a kiss perhaps... Then who knows? There was always a chance it might lead to something more, something he'd been aching for, for a long time, things he so acutely knew were missing from his life. Warmth, companionship, a friend he could open up to, a chance to feel needed... Maybe even loved.

"Go on then…" He took a tentative step forward onto the concrete strip that separated him from what he so desperately wanted. The cracked surface of the narrow one-way street now seemed as wide as the Grand Canyon, and just as formidable to cross. But cross it he must, and when he reached the other side he'd simply push his way through the door and join the throng of people inside. What could be so difficult about that?

Edward had been in Los Angeles for only four weeks, but his hometown of Ellingsworth, North Carolina, already seemed a distant place, both in miles and in his memories. He'd wanted to get out of Ellingsworth so badly he could almost taste the freedom it would bring him. When he'd finally cut himself loose from his so-called friends and family, it had been with such little regret that he still marveled at how easy it had been in the end.

After finally making the supreme effort to cross the street, he stood staring at the door of the Rockin' Bar, closed against the chill of the night air. All he had to do was push it open and he could enter into the warmth he was sure awaited him on the other side. The decision was taken out of his hands when two young guys brushed past him, swung the door open, and one of them, giving Edward a sweet smile, held it for him.

"Th-thanks…" He grabbed the handle then followed them inside. Edward had only ever been in one gay bar before, and that had been in Charlotte, North Carolina, a city as different from Los Angeles as beer is from champagne. Edward couldn't quite believe just how big a space the bar encompassed—it was at least half a football field long—and there was an upper floor—and everywhere there were people—mostly men, standing practically shoulder to shoulder or dancing on the huge wooden floor in the center of the bar. The noise was incredible. A wall of sound surrounded him. Laughter, chatter and the thump, thumping bass he'd only been vaguely aware of outside on the street now overwhelmed his senses, made him feel vibrant... *Alive*.

He headed for the bar where the bartender, a hottie wearing shorts and a big smile, asked him, "What'll it be, handsome?"

"You have Stella?"

"On tap, just for you, my pretty. Small or large?"

"Maybe a small one, to start." The bartender's sunny smile and flirty attitude went a long way to make Edward relax and feel glad he'd made the decision to get out and test the waters of LA's gay scene.

"On the house." The bartender placed a glass of amber liquid in front of Edward. "Name's Gary by the way."

"Edward — and thanks for the beer."

They shook hands across the bar. "Pleasure. Like to look after our first timers, so you'll come back."

Edward had no doubt he'd come back. When Gary left to take care of his other customers, Edward took a long swig of his Stella, savoring the refreshing coolness and slightly nutty taste. He glanced around the bar, avoiding too much eye contact with the other patrons, but taking in the general mix of guys his own age and some older men talking, smiling, laughing in groups or couples, or simply standing alone, like himself. Despite the volume of music there was a mellow ambience present in the bar, and even the need to shout to be heard wasn't overly irritating. He couldn't help but compare these people with the grim faces he'd left behind.

After months of muttered innuendo directed his way in the workplace, unreturned phone calls from those he'd once considered friends, silence and hard stares from his parents, bullying taunts and punches from his brother, he'd had enough. The job he'd applied for on the Internet had seemed at first to be a bit of a stretch for him. It had meant relocation, new surroundings, no one he knew nearby—daunting prospects without a doubt—but wasn't that exactly what he'd wanted? To shake himself free of the depression that had dogged him night and day, the inner loneliness he had felt sure would consume him completely and lead him to do something really stupid, like end his life, all because he was seen to be different in the eyes of those around him.

But was he really so different? Hadn't he seen on the TV masses of people like him celebrating the overturning of Proposition 8 in California, the legalization of same-sex marriage in sixteen states, the end of DOMA and DADT? The world was changing, and Edward wanted to be a part of that change, wanted recognition for himself, what he was, who he was. More than anything he wanted to find another like himself, someone who would understand him, love him unconditionally just as he would love in return.

Well, that wasn't going to happen in Ellingsworth, North Carolina—a too-small town where everyone knew not only your name but everything else about you, too. Where it was considered only right to correct what they perceived to be wrong, no matter who it hurt, no matter the fallout. When Edward, buoyed by the progress he could see all around the country, had come out to his family, he truly had not expected the hateful reaction he'd received.

They hadn't thrown him out, but it might have been better if they had. His father had told him to never mention such a hideous thing again, never to tell anyone else of his *perversion*, and to pray nightly to God for deliverance from his sinful ways. However, his brother, Craig, wasn't satisfied with his family's judgment. He'd made it his business to let everyone they knew in on Edward's confession. Even his father's wrath couldn't shut Craig up, and before long Edward had found himself ostracized by just about everyone he came in contact with. The world might be changing, but not Edward's world, not in Ellingsworth, North Carolina. His decision to leave had been met with indifference both at home and where he worked at the local bank. He'd had a feeling the manager was getting ready to fire him anyway, after being informed of Edward's *unnatural tendencies*. Yes, brother Craig had done an excellent job of character assassination.

Thanks, bro, hope I never have to look at your acne-ridden face again...

In order to shake off the depressing effects of too much reminiscing about the shit he'd hopefully left behind, he downed the last of his drink and walked to the edge of the dance floor. He felt filled with the sudden need to become one with the music, to dance, to give his body over to the rhythm, to let it all take him away from past regret and dismal memories.

"Wanna dance?" A tousled-haired, smiling vision appeared before him, shirtless, his skin covered completely in ink. Dragons and serpents seemed to writhe on the man's bare flesh under the colored lights that flashed overhead. Edward stepped back, startled and a little put off by the guy's bizarre appearance. An overabundance of tattoos on anyone had never been his thing. If he wanted to read quotations or look at pictures, he'd buy a book. But he had no time to say no, or even think, as his would-be dance partner tugged him onto the floor and immediately spun him into a sweaty, muscular embrace.

"Haven't seen you here before." The man had to shout, his lips on Edward's ear to be heard over the music.

"My first time," Edward yelled back. They were dancing so close he had no choice but to put his hands, reluctantly, on the guy's tattooed, and sweat-sticky shoulders.

"I'm Herbie."

"Edward."

"I come here most every night," Herbie told him. "I love to dance."

"You're good," Edward said, and he was. Edward loved to dance too, and he responded without effort to Herbie's undulating rhythm, their bodies moving to the pounding beat. But Edward couldn't help but be uncomfortably aware of the press of Herbie's crotch against his own or the fact that Herbie had slid his hands down to cover Edward's butt, squeezing hard, holding him firmly in place as he ground his hips over Edward's. Edward felt uneasy with this amount of intimacy from someone he hadn't known existed until a few seconds ago. He didn't want to be rude, or make his unease too apparent, but when Herbie planted an open-mouthed, tongue-wriggling kiss on his lips, he decided this was going way too far, way too fast, and he wasn't enjoying it one iota.

He jerked his head away and tried to squirm out of Herbie's arms. "You need to slow down, mister."

"We're just getting started." Herbie laughed and tightened his arms around Edward's waist.

"No, we're just getting over it." Edward was thankful at that moment for the hours he spent working out every week. He knew he was stronger than his five ten, one hundred and sixty pound frame suggested, and Herbie gasped with surprise when Edward suddenly pushed him backwards, and he almost ended up on his ass.

"Hey! That's not very nice."

"You're right, and neither is trying to stick your tongue down my throat less than a minute after asking me to dance."

They were yelling at each other over the pounding of the music, which chose that moment to quieten down for a segue into a slower tune. Edward felt his face heat up with embarrassment. *Jeez. First night out and I'm causing a fucking scene!*

"What are you—some kind of prude?" Herbie, obviously not at all embarrassed, just pissed off, continued to yell at him.

"No, I'm someone with taste." *Not terrific but it's the best I can do right now.*

"Oh, la-di-fucking-da," Herbie sneered and stomped off, soon lost among the throng of dancers. The majority of whom, Edward thankfully noted, didn't seem to care about his little fracas.

Well, damn, maybe I was rude using the 'taste' jab, but hell, he really was obnoxious trying to pull a stunt like that.

He headed back to the bar, relieved to see Gary still there, still smiling, and a knowing expression on his cute face.

"Ready for another?"

"More than ready. Make it a large one this time."

Gary chuckled. "Pay no attention to Herbie, he's a pain in the ass. He has to ask the new guys to dance 'cause nobody else gives him the time of day. He's what you might call *persistent*."

Edward watched the flex of Gary's biceps as he pulled on the draft handle and filled the beer glass to the brim with frothy amber liquid. Edward licked his lips in anticipation, an action not missed by Gary who winked and said, "Can't say I blame Herbie for wanting a taste of those luscious lips."

Edward pushed a ten over the bar. "I guess I'm not used to people coming on to me so fast."

"Really?" Gary raised one well-shaped eyebrow. "Where've you been hiding yourself – a monastery?"

"No, Ellingsworth, North Carolina."

"Never heard of it."

"You're lucky."

"So how long have you been in LA?"

"Four weeks. This is the first time I've actually been out, apart from going to see a couple of movies."

"And you have to run into Herbie. Helluva first impression."

Edward chuckled. "I'll get over it."

"You look like you can take care of yourself anyway."

"When you have an older brother who gets his kicks from beating up on you, you learn how to defend yourself real fast – or how to cover the bruises."

Gary threw him a quick glance of sympathy before he had to go take care of some impatient customers yelling for service, but came back a few moments later, complete with his open, sunny smile, and a message. "See the guy standing at the end of the bar to your right?"

Edward nodded after taking what he hoped was a surreptitious look, one just long enough to take in the fact that the guy was tall with a hot Latin appearance… Spanish or Italian, perhaps.

"Yes, I see him."

"Wants to buy you a drink. He'd like you to join him, he says."

"Do you know him?" Edward asked.

"He's been in a couple of times. Hard to miss with those exotic looks. Good tipper too, but that's about as much as I know." He winked at Edward. "Don't worry, I'll keep an eye out in case he tries a Herbie on you."

Edward laughed. "Okay, guess I'm safe enough then if you've got my back."

Gary grinned but didn't make any lewd follow-up remark. "Enjoy," was all he said.

The man at the end of the bar was drinking red wine and raised his glass as Edward approached, slowly winding his way through the milling crowd. He was momentarily stunned by just how good-looking the man appeared. Older than him, Edward guessed, late twenties maybe. He wore a T-shirt and jeans, both black, and sufficiently tight to show off his lean, muscular body to great advantage.

"Hello." The hottie smiled. "I'm Alex Martinez."

"Edward Conway." They shook hands, and Edward liked the cool, firm grip. He took in the dark brown eyes framed by sooty lashes, the aquiline nose, full lower lip and the white, even teeth his smile revealed. He eyed the almost full glass in Edward's hand.

"I'd like to buy you a drink, but I see you have one."

"That's okay," Edward said, then surprised himself by adding, "I'm happy to just talk, if that's all right with you."

"Very all right, although it's tough to do in here with all the noise." He took a sip of his wine and his dark eyes held a hint of humor as he gazed at Edward over the rim of his glass. "I liked the way you handled the tattooed gentleman on the dance floor."

Edward grimaced. "You saw that? I don't usually get into confrontations so easily—especially within minutes of coming into a bar for the first time. Gary, the bartender, told me Herbie's a bit on the pushy side with first timers."

"Herbie—that's right. Couldn't remember his name. He came on to me too, the first time I was here."

"Can't say I blame him for trying," Edward remarked with a wry smile.

"I like your accent, very Southern gentleman. Are you from Virginia?"

"North Carolina. You won't have heard of the town."

"Try me."

"Ellingsworth."

"You're right, I haven't heard of it."

They chuckled together and Edward relaxed under the warmth of Alex's charismatic personality.

"You like the Rockin' Bar?" Alex asked.

"Yeah. I read in a magazine this was one of the best dance bars in LA so I had to check it out."

"Ah, so you like to dance?"

"Love it. How about you?"

"Are you asking me to dance?"

Edward jerked his head in the direction of the dance floor. "Never can resist Radiohead," he said, grinning.

"Let's do it." Alex grabbed Edward's hand and together they eased their way through the crowd.

Maybe this evening won't be a dud after all. Edward took time to admire Alex's tall frame from behind and get an eyeful of the round contours of his muscular butt. The awkward moment with Herbie was forgotten as he and Alex joined the gyrating throng on the floor. Alex placed his hands lightly on Edward's hips and started to move expertly to the solid beat. *Oh yeah...* He followed Alex's lead, matching the man's sensuous moves. They shared a smile then Alex pulled him closer and leaned in to brush his lips lightly over Edward's.

Wow, twice in one night... More than I've had in so long I can't remember. And this time I don't mind it at all. Nice... Better than nice.

He felt a definite stirring in his groin from Alex's featherlight touch and the thought of protesting as he had with Herbie didn't even cross his mind. Instead, he pushed forward a little, inviting more than just a touch, parting his lips slightly. He breathed out an involuntary gasp when Alex slid the tip of his tongue over his lower lip. The thrill of it sent a jolt of desire straight to Edward's cock. Wanting to prolong the sensation of Alex's mouth on his, he reached up to cup the nape of Alex's neck, holding him in place as their tongues tangled and the kiss morphed from one of mere fleeting pleasure to mind melting ecstasy.

He was only vaguely aware that the music had slowed, and with it the movement of Alex's body, now firmly pressed against Edward's. Alex wrapped his strong arms around him, and an unmistakable hardness glided over his own confined erection. He leaned back just a little when their kiss ended so he could gaze into Alex's dark brown eyes. They met his own with an intensity so powerful it made him tremble with anticipation of what the rest of this evening might bring. He'd never done this before, never allowed such searing intimacy with a veritable stranger, yet it seemed so natural. So good... So right. He inhaled the intoxicating, spicy scent that lingered on the smooth skin of Alex's neck and buried his face there.

They were barely moving now, simply swaying sensuously to the music, then Alex asked, "Perhaps we could find somewhere quieter to talk?"

"Sounds like a plan." Although he hated to give up the pleasure of being in Alex's arms, the prospect of spending more time with him, perhaps alone, had the greater edge. There was no doubt from the state of both their arousals that talking would lead to something even more satisfying. At least that's what he hoped for... Maybe at last fulfilling his fantasy.

"I'm going to have to visit the john," he said when they returned to the bar. "That beer is going straight through me. Sorry."

Alex smiled. "I'll be right here when you get back. Don't get lost."

"I won't." He headed toward the restroom sign. There was no one at the urinals but muffled sounds and whispers from one of the stalls told him he wasn't alone. He'd just unzipped when he heard the main door open behind him.

"Quite a display you were putting on back there," a hostile sounding voice echoed off the tiled walls. Edward glanced round to see Herbie leaning against the sink counter, glaring at him. "Your refined *taste* doesn't exclude the likes of Alex Martinez, then?"

"You know him?"

"You sound surprised. Why shouldn't I know him? You think he's too hot for me to be acquainted with?"

"No, I don't think that at all." Edward finished, tucked himself back in his jeans and zipped up. "I really don't know why we're having this conversation, though." He strode over to one of the sinks, as far from Herbie as possible, and rinsed his hands under the hot water. "It's none of your business who I dance with."

"Or who you practically have sex with on the dance floor. The hick, country boy from Bumfuck, North Carolina, becomes a slut when—"

"Excuse me?" Edward cut Herbie off and took a step closer toward him. Edward might be new in town but he wasn't going to be intimidated by anyone's bullying tactics—gay or straight. Herbie backed up a tad but gave him a pugnacious stare. "Look…" Edward took a breath to calm down. "I'm sorry if I overreacted on the dance floor, but I didn't know you from Adam—and I didn't think it was okay for you to grope my ass and stick your tongue down my throat two seconds after we met."

"Is that right? I didn't see you complaining when fuckin' Alex Martinez was doing the same thing." Herbie crossed his arms and once again it appeared as if some of the tattooed monsters on his skin had come to life.

Bizarre…

Edward controlled his revulsion and the impulse to punch the derision right off Herbie's face. "Like I said, I don't know why we're talking about this. It's none of your damn business, but if you don't shut up, right now, I will forget my *country boy* good manners and slap that stupid sneer from your face." He turned to leave, then asked, "How the hell d'you know I'm from North Carolina?"

"Apart from the hick accent you mean? Gary, the bartender, told me. He thought you were so sweet. Man, did he get a shock when he saw you grinding against Martinez like a bitch in heat."

Edward laughed. "And you're calling *me* a hick? Get a life, Herbie. This is a gay bar, where the sight of two guys kissing on the dance floor doesn't exactly shake up the bartender."

"Yeah, well you're getting in over your head. Martinez is some kind of big—" Herbie quickly shut up when the restroom door opened and Alex stood framed in the doorway.

"Is everything all right?" he asked Edward. "You've been gone a long time."

"Everything's fine." Edward chuckled. "Herbie here was trying to interest me in getting tattoos like his. But I have to say, if I never see them again, that'll suit me just fine." "Shall we go then?" Alex opened the door a little more. "I have a place in mind where we can actually hear one another."

"Sounds good. 'Night, Herbie."

"Fuckers," Herbie muttered and stomped off ahead of them.

Alex put an arm round Edward's shoulders. "What happened?"

"Oh, he's pissed that I objected to him trying to put the make on me earlier. He'll get over it."

"Yes, he will." There was a determined set to Alex's mouth and Edward sensed he should head off any kind of impending confrontation between the two men.

"Uh, let's not add any more unpleasantness, and just go."

"If you're sure you're all right."

"I'm fine."

Alex closed the restroom door and pushed Edward against it. "You certainly are," he murmured before taking Edward's lips in another long kiss. The tension fell from Edward's body and he slid his arms up and around Alex's neck, holding him, savoring his taste. The kiss became hotter and Edward was on the brink of lifting Alex's T-shirt to get at his skin when a strangled groan came from the occupied stall. He'd forgotten they weren't quite alone.

"Not here," Alex whispered, his lips still on Edward's.

Edward chuckled and rested his forehead on Alex's. "Definitely not here."

* * * *

After they had said goodnight to Gary, and Edward had received a thumbs-up from the bartender, they stepped outside into the chill night air.

"I should've brought a jacket," Edward mumbled and pressed himself into Alex's side.

"My car's right there," Alex said, putting an arm round Edward's waist and hurrying him forward. "Where are you parked?"

"I took a cab. Where are we going?"

"My place."

"Oh…"

"Too pushy?" The lights on his car, a white BMW, blinked and Alex opened the passenger door. "I promise nothing will happen that you don't want to. But it is quieter, and I'd like to spend some time with you alone."

"Uh, okay, but can you drop me off at my place, after?"

"Of course."

Edward got in the car, trying to ignore the flutter of nerves in his stomach. Alex seemed very nice, protective even, and sexy as hell. But appearances could be deceptive. He knew that only too well from experience, and what little experience he had wasn't anything he really wanted to remember. Well, if things went wrong he could always leave. He might have to get a cab home, but he could handle that.

"I have to tell you I haven't done this before," he said as Alex put the car in gear and they pulled out onto the road. "I mean, go back to a guy's place after just meeting him. Of course, the chances of that happening when I lived at home were pretty remote. The couple of times I went into Charlotte I was too nervous to really enjoy myself. There was always the chance that I'd run into someone I knew."

"But wouldn't running into someone you knew be a good thing?" Alex asked.

"In what way?"

"Well, you'd know you weren't alone. You could make friends."

"Friends. Yeah that would've been nice. I had some friends once."

"What happened?"

"Life, I guess."

Alex gave him a sidelong glance. "You are far too young to be so cynical, Edward."

"Your accent," Edward said suddenly. "It's faint, but I hear it now and then. Are you Spanish?"

"Puerto Rican. The Alex is short for Alejandro. Alex makes it easier for people to remember."

"I would definitely remember Alejandro. It's a beautiful name. Better than Edward, don't you think? And I really hate it when people shorten it to Ed or Eddie."

Alex chuckled quietly. "Edward is a perfectly good name—and all that interest in my accent was a none too subtle way of changing the subject."

"Sorry, but I really don't like talking about what I once had. I'm here, in LA now, and I want to look forward, not backward."

Alex nodded. "Perhaps when we know each other better, you'll find it easier to tell me about it."

"Shit, I'm sorry." Edward put his hand on Alex's thigh and rubbed it gently. "Was I being rude? I didn't intend to be."

Alex covered Edward's hand with his own. "No, you weren't rude—just guarded. And that's understandable. You've only known me for a couple of hours."

Edward sighed. "That's right, and I have to admit I am nervous about going home with you—yet at the same time it feels kind of *good*, being with you. Better than I've felt in a long time."

"I'm glad." He squeezed Edward's hand. "Listen, if you'd rather not come back to my place tonight, I'll understand. We can make arrangements to meet another night. Tomorrow I'm free, then I'm flying to New York on business. I'll be gone for about four days."

Edward stared at Alex and couldn't quite control the sinking feeling in his stomach. *Why, when I've just met the guy?* Even though he'd be the first to say that yes, he was nervous about going back with Alex to his place—despite that, he was looking forward to what their time alone might bring. He didn't really want to wait until tomorrow night.

"No, it's okay." He was surprised his voice sounded steady and sure. "I'd like to go home with you tonight, if you don't mind. I mean if…if you're still in the mood. Uh…"

Alex chuckled and squeezed Edward's hand again. "I'm in the mood to get to know you better. Here we are." He pulled into a driveway, at the end of which stood a modest-looking, white stucco house. They got out of the car and walked the few steps to the front door, which Alex unlocked then stepped aside so that Edward could enter.

Chapter Two

The interior was larger than he would have guessed from the outside. Wooden floors stretched the length of the living room, and through the French doors at the far end, Edward could see the soft blue reflection of light on water. A swimming pool. Not something he'd be tempted to try out on this chilly night, unfortunately. An arched fireplace surrounded by an intricate pattern of river stones took up the majority of one wall while the others held some large framed pieces of modern art.

"Make yourself comfortable." Alex pointed at the overstuffed leather couch in front of the fireplace. "Would you like a beer, or something else to drink?"

"Beer's fine, thanks." Edward felt a little in awe of Alex's home. Everything appeared to be *expensive*, and so very different from the house he'd been raised in, and the now meager apartment he shared with two roommates. While his host went into the kitchen to fetch his beer, he did a slow turn around, taking it all in before sinking down onto the couch's plump cushions. He thought about what Alex must do for a living that afforded him such a beautiful place, and took him to New York for meetings. Something high powered, no doubt, and very different from being a bank teller. It was obvious their lives were poles apart, and he wondered why on earth Alex had chosen him to befriend when he could so easily have just about anyone he fancied.

He should be flattered, but what he felt was unease and the sad realization that this could only be for one night, if it even went that far. *But he did say he is free tomorrow night and they could meet.* He looked up as Alex came back into the living room, a glass of beer in one hand, and wine in the other.

"You seem to be deep in thought," he remarked, sitting down beside Edward and handing him his beer.

"Just admiring this room. It's very nice."

"This house belonged to my aunt." He took a sip of his wine before continuing. "She left it to me when she passed two years ago. It's an old California home — they don't build them like this anymore."

"So your family's lived in California a long time?"

"Maria, my aunt, married a guy with a construction business here in LA. Their marriage didn't last, but she liked California so she stayed. I would come here on vacation, then when my mother died I moved in with my aunt."

"I'm sorry — about your mother I mean."

"Thank you. It was many years ago. I was just a kid, ten years old, though I do have some nice memories of her." He took Edward's hand. "And you... You have a family back in North Carolina?"

"Yes, but I'm afraid there are no nice memories. Some okay memories. My mom and I got along fine until…" He sighed. "Well, I said I didn't want to talk about it."

"It might help if you share. Get it off your chest. I can tell you are harboring some bitter regrets."

He lifted Edward's hand to his lips and kissed it gently. Edward gazed into the man's dark eyes and for the first time in so long, he couldn't remember precisely when it was, he experienced a surge of happiness, mixed with lust. But what exactly was wrong with having both those feelings at the same time? *A happy lust.* It felt good. Just being here with Alex felt good. So different from the previous times he'd been with a guy, even a guy he'd wanted to be with…

But don't get too caught up in it. Mustn't put too much emphasis beyond the fact that Alex seems like a really nice guy. More than merely handsome, and sitting so close, holding my hand and making me forget the misgivings I had earlier about being alone with him here in his home.

"There you go again," Alex said, his deep voice a balm to Edward's ears. "So lost in thought. So many emotions churning inside you. Relax, Edward. You don't have to tell me anything you don't want to — or do anything you don't absolutely want to."

Forcing his nervousness away, Edward whispered, "What I'd really like is to kiss you again."

Alex took Edward's glass and placed it along with his wine glass on the low table in front of the couch. "I think I'd like that too," he murmured before taking Edward into his arms. "You have a very kissable mouth."

"You—" Edward was about to return the compliment but his voice was stilled by the pressure of Alex's warm, soft lips on his and he let himself be lost in the sensual pleasure of the moment.

* * * *

When Alex had first seen the slim, blond young man standing at the bar, he'd had a moment of déjà vu. Seven years had passed since he'd met Hank, and there was something about Edward that reminded him of Hank. Not so much physically, beyond the fact that they were both blond and blue-eyed — more perhaps in the way he felt drawn to Edward just as he had been drawn to Hank, all those years ago. That chance encounter in another bar, another time, had resulted in his going home with Hank — and never leaving for over five years, until that fateful night when his whole world had been turned upside down, and he'd thought it would never be all right again.

He didn't want to think about Hank right then. There was still too much pain involved in those memories. And now — was it too soon to be doing this — holding this extremely good-looking young man in his arms and kissing him like there was no tomorrow? But the kisses were definitely having a blurring effect on his reasoning, especially as Edward gave back as good as he was getting. Edward's lips were warm and soft and succulent, and his tongue that he had at first pressed shyly against the seam of Alex's lips too enticing to resist. Alex opened to him and their tongues glided and tangled and explored every hot, moist corner of each other's mouths.

Their kiss deepened and Alex could sense a kind of desperation in Edward, as if he hadn't had this kind of intimacy before, or at least for a long time. The way he clung to him, almost like he was afraid Alex would suddenly pull back and end their embrace. He tightened his arms around Edward. If he was right about Edward's apprehension, he wanted to assure him there was no danger of that happening. However uncertain he was of his own emotions, he instinctively knew Edward needed this, and Alex wasn't about to be the one to disappoint him.

After gently breaking their kiss, he undid the buttons of Edward's shirt then brushed his lips over the smooth skin he had exposed. Edward shivered and an almost inaudible gasp escaped him.

Alex ran his thumb lightly over Edward's lower lip. "Have you not done this before?"

"Not with someone like you."

"Someone like me?" Alex smiled. "What does that mean?"

The blue gaze Edward cast at Alex was achingly earnest. "Someone as—as *handsome* as you." It was obvious to Alex from the shadowed expression on Edward's face that although he was making light of his answer, this emotionally vulnerable young man harbored some bad memories. "This is the first time I've felt—" Edward looked away and his cheeks flushed scarlet.

"It's okay," Alex said softly. "Tell me what you're feeling."

Edward looked back at him. "Like this is perfect, you know? The way I always thought it would, *should* be. Being held and kissed with no sign of—of disgust or shame afterward."

"Disgust?" Alex couldn't keep the shock out of his voice. "How on earth could anyone be disgusted by you?" He cupped Edward's face within his hands and kissed the corner of Edward's mouth. "You are a beautiful young man, Edward, and so far from disgusting I can't imagine anyone thinking otherwise.

Only if they were perhaps ashamed and disgusted with themselves, but that's their problem, not yours."

"Unfortunately, they made it my problem, but—" He dropped his gaze again. "I'm spoiling things with my whining. I don't know why I said all of that in the middle of what we were doing."

"*Are* doing," Alex said, smiling. "We're not going to stop any time soon, if you don't want to."

"Oh, God, I don't want you to—stop, that is."

"Okay, where was I?" Alex gave a deep chuckle. "Ah yes, I was about to lick those perky little nipples of yours." He leaned in to do just that, but as even as he enjoyed feasting on the tiny hard nubs he made a mental note to encourage Edward to talk more of his past, and perhaps help him put to rest some of the demons that apparently still troubled him.

Edward moaned, his body writhing from the sensations that coursed through him at the sensuous touch of Alex's lips and tongue. He'd known from the brief kiss they'd shared on the dance floor that he wanted to have sex with this man. Sex that for the first time he could really lose himself in without the threat of scary repercussions. Without flinching from the harsh words and rough actions that had followed his abortive few attempts to find pleasure with another man. There was nothing remotely threatening about Alex—except that if he kept on kissing and caressing Edward so expertly there was danger all right. He would come far too quickly and the exquisite thrill of being with this—was it too sappy to even think it?— *dream come true*, would be over long before he was ready. A whimper escaped his throat and he grabbed the hand unbuckling his belt.

Alex raised his head, his expression questioning.

"I, I want you to, but I'm afraid I-I'll come—"

Alex chuckled. "I'd be disappointed if you didn't."

"But not so soon."

"Just relax. Enjoy." He nuzzled again at Edward's nipples then kissed his way over Edward's abdomen, stopping just short of the belt buckle. He glanced up with a teasing smile and slowly undid first the belt, then the zipper. Edward gulped on a sharp intake of breath. He didn't think his erection could get any harder, but as Alex traced the bulging outline of the rigid length with his lips, through the white cotton of Edward's briefs, he felt as if it might have done just that. His body trembled with anticipation and his heart hammered so loudly, the sound thrummed in his ears.

He almost came off the couch at the first touch of Alex's lips on the head of his cock. Alex took all of him in one long smooth glide right down to the base. The effect was like nothing Edward had felt before. The moist heat that surrounded his pulsing shaft, the sensuous sensation of Alex's tongue stroking him up and down brought a scalding surge straight into his balls.

"Oh, God…" He delved his fingers into Alex's thick hair as much to caress as to warn him he was losing control—the danger was imminent. "*Alex*." He squirmed, trying to get away, but Alex held him tight and increased the power of his sucking, taking him into the depths of his throat. Edward let out a hoarse cry, arching his body into his orgasm, powerless to hold back any longer. His mind went into free fall, the darkness behind his tightly closed eyes suddenly shot through with a brilliant kaleidoscope of colors. He gasped and shuddered in the throes of the most amazing climax he'd ever experienced made even more mind-blowing by Alex's persistence in holding him in his mouth and draining every drop from him.

As he slowly wound down from his high, Alex traced a tingling trail of kisses up Edward's torso until he reached his mouth, then settled a long, languorous kiss on his lips.

"Okay?" he whispered when he pulled back slightly.

"Okay?" Edward repeated, widening his eyes. "That was—well, it was totally incredible. I've never come like that before, and I'm sorry, I tried to warn you but—"

"Shush…" Alex put a finger over Edward's lips. "You did nothing I didn't also want. You taste delicious, by the way."

"I'd like to return the favor," Edward said shyly. He slipped his hands under the T-shirt Alex still wore, and ran his hands over the man's muscular back.

"Mmm… I think we should get out of these clothes, don't you? Maybe make use of the bed. Would you like that?"

Edward nodded. "Very much."

"Good." Alex rose and stretched his long, lean body like a cat. He held out a hand to Edward. "Come on then. Let me lead you to my lair."

Edward took the proffered hand and stood up. "Your lair—sounds exciting."

"That's what I'm going for." He hooked an arm round Edward's waist and led him toward a door on the far side of the living room. "Oh, can I get you something to drink?"

"Maybe just some water."

"I'll go get a couple of bottles. Let me just turn on a light for you." He pushed the door open and flipped a switch on the wall, bathing the room in a soft glow. "There— Don't start without me."

Edward chuckled. "No chance of that happening." He glanced around the room and again was impressed with the size and the stylish décor, but mostly with the king-size bed covered in a richly patterned comforter. *Wow, this is so nice*. He shucked off his shirt and threw it onto a nearby chair. He sat down to remove his shoes and socks, then slipped out of his jeans. He kept his briefs on, feeling just a little unsure about stripping down to the buff. *Funny really after what we've been doing*. But his innate shyness still made him hesitate to stand around in the nude without Alex there to encourage him.

"Here we go." Alex hurried in carrying two bottles of water, one of which he gave to Edward. "Mmm, you have one fine body," he added, eyeing Edward's physique up and down and making him squirm under the scrutiny. "Don't blush. You work out. You know what you've got there." He ran a hand over Edward's hard abs. "Very nice." He leaned in to suck on Edward's left nipple. Edward could feel his second arousal building inside him, hardening his cock again. But he couldn't just stand there and let Alex do all the work again. More than anything, he wanted to see what that black T-shirt only hinted at.

"Let me." He slipped his hands under the hem of the tee and tugged it upwards while Alex raised his arms to let Edward pull the shirt over his head. Edward flung it on top of his clothes then directed his attention to the lithe, muscular contours of Alex's chest and abdomen. "Beautiful," he murmured, running a finger between Alex's pectoral muscles then circling each nipple before flicking his tongue over the tiny nubs. Alex moaned and caressed the back of Edward's head. Edward licked and kissed his way down Alex's solidly muscled torso then knelt before him and pressed his lips to the hard bulge behind the fabric of Alex's jeans. He trembled with breathless anticipation as he undid the button fly then inched the denim down over Alex's slim hips.

This was so different from the time when he'd given his first blow job and the man had grabbed him painfully by the hair and forcibly jammed him face first into his hairy groin then pushed his hardness into Edward's mouth, forcing it down his throat, making him gag and splutter with revulsion. Now, Edward had the pleasurable feeling that he was in control, that with Alex there would be no crude power-play or unwanted demands made upon him.

He released Alex's hard shaft from the confines of his briefs and held it in both hands. He gazed at it for a few moments to admire its girth and upward curve then he caressed the silky skin, relishing the powerful pulsing he felt in his grip. He leaned in to kiss the head, rubbing the pre-cum at the slit over his lips. Slowly, sensually, he brought the head of Alex's shaft into his mouth.

A long, throaty moan escaped Alex and he wound his fingers through Edward's hair. Edward looked up, and to his delight saw that Alex's eyes were closed, his expression one of apparent ecstasy. His hips bucked forward, and Edward sucked the thick length all the way into his mouth, his tongue swirling over the throbbing flesh until he reached the root and its thatch of dark hair. He buried his nose in the scent of Alex's maleness, the slightly spicy musk filling his senses, causing his own cock to harden again to an almost painful degree. He pulled back, almost releasing the head from his mouth before gliding back down, at the same time cupping Alex's firm butt and pulling him in even deeper so he could clench his throat muscles round the tip of Alex's shaft.

Alex shuddered and Edward knew he was close. His excitement grew along with his anticipation of tasting Alex for the first time. He sucked long and hard, rolling his tongue over the ultrasensitive glans behind Alex's cockhead.

"Oh, Jesus, Edward, I'm coming!" The moan that sounded like it was torn from Alex's throat increased Edward's eagerness and he resisted Alex's attempt to draw back, holding him in place by wrapping his arms around Alex's hips. The first surge of semen on his soft palate took him by surprise, but he welcomed it and greedily swallowed as Alex emptied his balls into Edward's mouth.

Alex breathed out a long gasp, then lifting Edward to his feet, he took his lips in a long, ardent kiss that allowed them to share the salty taste.

"You are amazing," Alex murmured against Edward's lips. "For someone who says he hasn't done this very often, you give wonderful head."

"I..." Edward looked away for a moment, and his cheeks flamed. "I've watched a lot of porn."

Alex chuckled. "And I get the benefit of it, lucky me."

"I've never enjoyed it this much before."

Alex kissed him again. "Come on, let's lie on the bed so I can hold you properly." He stepped out of his jeans and briefs that were pooled around his feet and kicked them aside. He lifted Edward into his arms and Edward responded by holding on tight and wrapping his legs around Alex's hips. They shared another kiss as Alex walked them over to the bed. He sat down on the edge, Edward on his lap, the hard wedge of his cock probing the cleft between Edward's ass cheeks.

Edward shivered with desire. It was going to happen. Alex was going to fuck him and he couldn't be more excited—and more terrified.

You have to put the memories of the last time away, he told himself. *Thinking about that bastard could ruin everything.* And what he wanted more than anything was for it to be as perfect as it all had been up to this moment.

"You're nervous," Alex said, his lips on Edward's ear. "I told you nothing will happen that you don't want to happen."

"I do want it. I want you to fuck me. It's just that…"

"Bad experience?"

"Something like that, yes."

"Then we'll go slow, and if you tell me to stop, I will. I promise." He took Edward's lips again in a long, searing kiss. At the same time he fell back onto the bed with Edward on top then he rolled him onto his side, never breaking their kiss.

Edward was a mess of breathless expectation. He wanted this, almost to the point of desperation, but was he prepared for the agonizing pain he knew came as an inevitable part of being fucked—even by someone as beautiful as this man who now held him so protectively in his arms? Alex had said he'd go slow, and he was sure he could trust him to do just as he'd promised.

Alex eased him onto his back and began a slow and sensuous trail of kisses from Edward's mouth down his throat, over his chest, ravishing each nipple with lips and teeth until the tiny nubs tingled almost to the point of pain. Edward writhed under him, his body undulating with pleasure he'd only dreamt could be his. Never, even in his wildest fantasies, had he ever believed that one day a man would make love to him like this. Especially one as gorgeous as Alex. It was almost too good to be true. He was afraid to close his eyes in case this was just a dream and he would wake up and find himself alone in his rented room, Alex a mere figment of his imagination. But the warm, smooth skin and firm muscle under his hands were real all right, real enough to enflame him with an almost uncontrollable desire.

Alex shifted slightly in order to slip between Edward's legs. He gripped Edward's erection lightly at the base and Edward's breath hitched in his chest when he felt Alex's lips nuzzle his balls. He gasped when Alex sucked the delicate sac into his mouth, teasing each ball with his lips and tongue, the rush of ecstasy almost blinding in its intensity. That intensity was heightened when Alex trailed his tongue over the sensitive skin of Edward's perineum then lifted Edward's legs to gain access to the cleft between his buttocks. Edward fisted the sheets, trying to control the climax that threatened to overcome him at any moment. Alex circled Edward's pucker with the tip of his tongue then pushed past the ring of muscle guarding his hole, and Edward felt he might just come apart at the seams.

A hoarse cry of sheer, wanton pleasure was ripped from him as Alex continued to rim him, laving his opening with forceful probes that brought sensations Edward had never believed he'd ever experience. He'd only ever seen men do this in porn movies, had longed to know what it would feel like, but this—this beat all and any of his imaginings. The intensity increased when Alex inserted a finger along with his tongue, expertly finding Edward's prostate, massaging it gently.

Edward moaned and a veritable stream of pre-cum leaked from his cock, pooling in his navel. He thought he might lose control any moment so it was almost a relief when Alex pulled back then reached across to the nightstand. He felt a flutter of nerves in his stomach when he realized Alex was tearing open a condom packet. Watching as Alex eased the latex over the powerful upward curve of his cock, he bit down on his lower lip, trying to contain his anxiety. He wanted to enjoy this, but, perhaps even more importantly, he wanted Alex to enjoy it too, so that this wouldn't end up being just a one-night stand.

"Relax," Alex whispered and leaned down to kiss his lips gently. "You look tense. I promise if you don't like it I will stop. Don't try to be a hero and grin and bear it. This is something you should enjoy. It might hurt some at the beginning, but I'll go slow and it'll feel good, okay?

Edward nodded and encircled Alex's hips with his legs in acceptance. He shivered a little when Alex inserted a lubed finger inside him.

"Okay?"

"Yes. Feels nice. Real nice."

Alex moved his finger in and out in a gentle but firm rhythmic motion that had Edward pushing willingly against the erotic pressure of Alex's sure strokes. He put his hand behind Alex's head and pulled him in for a kiss. With Alex's lips on his he felt transported, sure he would experience nothing but pleasure when Alex entered him. Then the moment he'd been longing for with eager anticipation, mixed with not a little apprehension came when he felt the head of Alex's cock nudge at his opening then force its way past the ring of muscle that guarded his hole.

Oh shit, that hurts. He fought to control the wounded cry that rose in his throat and ended in a gasp into Alex's mouth. Alex paused and locked eyes with him.

"Tell me."

"It, it hurts, but I don't want you to pull out. I want this, Alex."

"Okay, try to relax a little more. I won't go in any further until you say I can. Just breathe and look at me."

Edward gazed up into the depths of Alex's dark brown eyes, seeing for the first time the tawny striations that circled the irises. *Beautiful,* he thought, *eyes I could drown in, lose myself, forget every bad thing that's ever happened.* He could feel the steady pulsing of Alex's cock inside him, see his smiling, lush mouth only inches from his own.

"Fuck me," he whispered and raised his hips, letting Alex slide all the way in. As ready as he thought he was, the intense burn as Alex's hard flesh impaled him made Edward's body stiffen with shock. Alex wrapped his arms around him more tightly and crooned softly in his ear.

"That's it, Edward, I won't move until you get used to me inside you. You feel wonderful, so hot and velvety smooth, just like I knew you would."

The words helped, along with the kisses Alex peppered along Edward's jaw from ear to ear before settling on his lips, his tongue gliding over Edward's in another searingly rapturous kiss.

"Oh, yes, it feels good, Alex. So good."

Now Alex began to move slowly, gently back and forth with a sensuousness that had Edward moaning with ecstasy. The pain was all but forgotten, the pleasure obliterating everything but the reality that this was what he had longed for, what he'd wanted more than anything, to feel at one with another man. Those disastrous couplings he'd endured while longing for someone who would raise him to these heights of ecstasy were forgotten under the power of Alex's tender yet passionate lovemaking.

He picked up on the rhythm Alex had created, slow at first, letting Edward feel the thick length inside him, each long thrust grazing his prostate, squeezing soft, breathy moans of ecstasy from him. He arched upwards, meeting every one of those sensual thrusts, pushing against Alex's driving force, drawing him deeper and deeper inside himself. Their bodies moved in perfect counterpoint, increasing in intensity, their breathing hot and harsh over each other's skin.

Alex grasped Edward's erection and began pumping it in unison with the now rapid rhythm they both moved to. Edward cried out from the pleasure Alex's touch brought him but he knew he couldn't hold out against this barrage of sensation. As much as he wanted this to last, to go on forever, he could feel the inevitable approach of climax. It swirled through the base of his spine, his balls pulled up tight and as the pressure built inside him, he shuddered and clutched desperately at Alex's broad shoulders.

"Yes, come for me," Alex whispered hoarsely and took Edward's mouth in a bruising kiss.

There was no more holding back. For just a second or two more he teetered on the knife edge of expectancy, then his orgasm rolled over him, flooding his senses with ecstasy. His cum spurted over Alex's hand, coating both their torsos with creamy heat.

Alex broke off their kiss long enough to croak, "Oh, God—I'm coming too."

Edward tightened his arms and legs around Alex and pushed his hips upwards relishing in the sensation of Alex's pulsing cock so deep inside him. Alex's sweat-slicked body vibrated under Edward's hands, and he could actually feel the heat of it when Alex flooded the condom with his semen. Alex collapsed over him then rolled them both over onto their sides so they were face to face, lips to lips, Alex still deep inside Edward.

"You okay?" Alex asked in a whisper.

"Very okay," Edward replied. He moved his hips, loving the pressure of Alex's cock. "That feels so good." He gave Alex a shy smile. "I enjoyed all of it, very much."

"I'm glad. As we say where I was born, *me gustó mucho*."

They lay curled together, legs and arms entwined, Edward resting his head on Alex's chest, Alex gently stroking Edward's hair. They were quiet, but the silence didn't feel uncomfortable to Edward — he was still enjoying the warm feeling of euphoria, the afterglow of having, for the first time in his life, sex that had completely fulfilled him. He only hoped that Alex had been honest when he'd said he'd enjoyed the sex — or it had been at least memorable.

Alex was the first to speak. "D'you have to work tomorrow?" he asked.

"Unfortunately, yes." Edward raised his head to glance at the digital clock on the nightstand. "And even more unfortunately, I should think about getting home."

"Yes, darn it." Alex hugged him and dropped a kiss on his forehead. "And I have an early morning meeting. We should get dressed and I'll take you back to your place."

"I'm sorry."

Alex put a finger on Edward's lips to still his apology. "Don't be. I told you I'd take you home when I asked you over here, and after what we've shared, it's the very least I can do." He smiled and kissed Edward gently on the lips. "To quote an old cliché, 'I hope it was as good for you as it was for me'."

"Good doesn't quite cover it," Edward said. "I only ever dreamed of having sex like this, I never thought it would ever happen." He looked up at Alex and sighed. "God, you must think I'm such a wimp, and a whiny one at that."

"Cut that out," Alex growled. "I don't think you're a wimp, or whiny. From what little you've told me, I realize you've been through some rough times. It's not always easy getting over the hurt caused by either family or friends. And like I told you, I'm here, ready to listen whenever you want to unload. Okay?"

"Thanks," Edward mumbled, but in the back of his mind he couldn't help but wonder why.

Why would this gorgeous man be even remotely interested in my problems?

* * * *

In the car Alex asked, "What is it you do exactly?"

"I'm a merchant teller, at Hastings Financial. It's not the greatest but I was lucky to secure the position before I came out to LA. And you? What do you do, Alex?"

"I work for the Scott Malone Agency. We handle publicity for celebrities, their press releases, arrange for interviews, that kind of thing."

"Sounds a lot more exciting than working in a bank. I bet you meet some really interesting people."

"It's not often dull, I'll grant you, but there are so-called celebrities who are far from interesting. Some are plain boring as a matter of fact."

"Really? That's hard to believe."

"Because you only see the sensational snippets of their lives that the tabloids exploit. If you got into a conversation with one or two of our clients you'd know what I'm talking about. Perhaps boring's a bit mean, but they can lead quite ordinary lives away from the cameras and spotlights."

"I don't think I could handle people prying into my private life," Edward said. "Sometimes I feel sorry for the way they're portrayed on the covers of those magazines I see at the supermarket checkouts—she's too fat, he's looking old. I even saw one headline where Kate was ready to throw William over for Harry!"

Alex chuckled. "And of course nine times out of ten it's all bullshit—especially stories like the ones you just mentioned."

"So they make them up?"

"A lot do. Then there are reporters and the paparazzi who scout for the real dirt. They can be dangerous at times."

Edward didn't miss the trace of bitterness in Alex's voice as he uttered those last words, but he had no time to question it as they had pulled up outside his apartment building and Alex had leaned over to kiss him gently on the lips.

"Goodnight, Edward. I'd like to see you again before I leave for New York."

"I'd like that too."

"Tomorrow then? I'll pick you up here at seven. We can have dinner together, okay?"

"Sounds wonderful. I'll be waiting for you out here at seven." He kissed Alex then reluctantly got out of the car. "See you tomorrow." He watched as Alex's car pulled away, did a quick U-turn then disappeared round the corner. His involuntary sigh voiced both disappointment and expectation. At least it wasn't going to be the one-night stand he'd feared in the beginning. He just wished he could make time stand still for a little longer and that this night wasn't yet over.

Chapter Three

Next day

The time at work seemed endless to Edward, and the long line of customers waiting for service never ending. But even the grouchiest client couldn't put a damper on his euphoric mood. All he had to do was to think back on the night before and relish the memory of being with Alex, plus the impending bonus of their date after he got off work. That, along with the pleasant ache in his butt, reminded him even more of the wonderful hours he'd spent with Alex. Just thinking about it made him hard and a slow heat infuse his neck and cheeks.

God, I really have to concentrate on what I'm doing. Still, he couldn't resist pressing his groin into the wooden drawer in front of him, and at the same time smiling at the old gentleman at his window who was making a deposit.

"You're in a good mood, young man," the old guy said. "Got some last night, did you?"

Edward couldn't contain the surprised laugh that bubbled up at the old man's remark. "Something like that," he replied through his laughter.

"That's the spirit. Gotta keep the engine tuned, well oiled and in fine working order."

"Absolutely. Will that be all?" Edward handed him his receipt.

"That'll do it." He gave Edward a sly grin. "Keep up the good work."

"I will. Have a nice day, sir."

Well, that's one conversation I never could have had in Ellingsworth. "Next in line, please."

* * * *

Back at his apartment he was glad to see neither of his roommates were home and the bathroom was free. Edward had replied to an online ad from two guys wanting to share their place with 'a gay or gay friendly employed person' and he'd been lucky to get the room. In the short space of time he'd lived here he hadn't really begun to know his 'roomies'. Troy and Kevin were both attractive young guys and pleasant enough, but they were rarely home, their jobs and social lives keeping them busy. On one of the rare occasions they were there together, Edward had learned that Troy worked for some big travel agency and Kevin was an accountant.

So far he hadn't hung out with either one, and in a way, although he sometimes felt lonely, he figured it was best to keep their arrangement uncomplicated. Kevin appeared pretty straightforward, but Edward felt a certain wariness around Troy. He couldn't quite put his finger on what it was exactly, just something that seemed a little off kilter—moodiness perhaps.

Alex had said he'd pick him up at seven then they'd go for a drink and get something to eat locally. While toweling himself off after his shower, he peered at his face in the mirror, searching for blemishes, and was pleased to find none. He was blessed with a fair, smooth skin and a light stubble that didn't really begin to show until two or three days without shaving. He'd shaved that morning, so it still felt okay under his probing fingers. He combed his blond hair back then spiked it up a little so it didn't look too 'preppy'. He spritzed on a little cologne then headed back to his room to finish dressing. The room had come furnished with the basics — good enough until he could afford perhaps a new comforter and maybe hang a couple of pictures to brighten up the place. It would never be anything as stylish as Alex's bedroom, but then not too many were. That he'd seen anyway.

He'd just pulled on his jeans when he heard the front door open and Troy, or maybe Kevin, yelling, "Hey, Ed, you have a visitor."

What the hell?

He practically stumbled out of his room, his eyes widening with surprise when he saw Alex standing in the living room.

"Sorry…" His date appeared to be only a little embarrassed. "I was early."

"I found him standing on the steps," Troy told him. "Being the nosy type that I am, I asked him if he was waiting for someone and he said Edward Conway, and I said that's my roommate, come on up. Hope it's okay," he added, clearly not caring if it was okay or not. "I'm Troy Kendall, by the way." He held out his hand.

"Alex Martinez." He took the proffered hand, pulling back when it seemed that Troy was holding on too long.

"Good to meet you." Troy smirked at Edward, then wandered off into the kitchen.

Edward stared at Alex for a moment or two, slightly tongue-tied. "Hi," he finally managed to say. "I-I'm almost ready."

Alex closed the gap between them and kissed him lightly. "You look wonderful."

"Thanks, you do too." He was wearing a charcoal-gray dress shirt and black tailored slacks that gave him an elegance and made Edward feel way underdressed.

"Are you upset at my being early? I decided to come straight from work as I was running a bit late." He gave Edward a disarming smile. "Hence the less than casual attire."

"No, it's great. I was just hoping to prepare you a bit before you saw this, uh…" He gestured at the room. "The guys aren't the tidiest and I didn't have a chance to clean up."

"No need to apologize. It's…uh, it's comfortable and — lived in." He leaned in for another kiss. "And you smell delicious." He wrapped his arms tightly around Edward. "I missed you today."

Edward felt his knees almost give way while his cock hardened from the sheer eroticism Alex exuded. He was so gorgeous and sexy, and not for the first time Edward wondered why he was single, and why so interested in him. When he opened his eyes after their kiss he saw Troy watching them, a beer can in hand, his expression a mixture of envy and disbelief.

Well, I can understand both those emotions, but he could be a mite more subtle.

"Uh, just let me put my shoes on and we can get going," he said quietly while slipping from Alex's embrace.

He hurried into his bedroom, pulled on the socks and shoes he'd laid aside earlier, took another quick peek at himself in the mirror, then with an impatient sigh, he flicked off the light and went back to the living room. Troy was sitting on the arm of the couch talking in a low but urgent tone and gazing up at Alex with an expression that Edward could only term as lecherous.

Shit, subtlety is definitely not in this guy's vocabulary. He was slightly mollified by the fact that Alex seemed to be staring over Troy's head, his lips twisted in a wry smile. He looked over at Edward and there was no mistaking the relief in his eyes as he grinned at him.

"There you are." He crossed the room quickly and took Edward's hand. "Shall we?"

Troy got to his feet, a surly cast to his face. "Well, nice meeting you—and uh, don't forget what I told you about, will you?"

"No, I certainly won't forget it," Alex replied, opening the door and practically pushing Edward into the hall outside. He shook his head and gave Edward a grim look. "Your roommate is something else."

"Was he trying to put the make on you? I don't blame him, but I can't believe he'd do it right in front of me."

"Not only that, he invited me to a party over the weekend some friends of his are throwing—lots of drugs and sex he said, waggling his eyebrows at me, like he thought I'd find that sexy."

"Jeez." Edward shook his head. "Wait. Did you?"

"Did I what?"

"Find it sexy."

Alex snorted. "No." Just before they reached the main door out to the street, he grabbed Edward's arm and tugged him into a fast embrace. "Troy is quite attractive, I suppose, but there was just one guy in the room I found sexy." He kissed Edward's lips then said, "You."

"Thanks. I saw him watching us when you were kissing me. I could tell by his expression he was pissed, like he couldn't believe I was getting what he wanted."

Alex pushed his groin against Edward's, grinding their erections together. "Well, he's not getting any of this. I don't go any place where there's drugs and I'm not into orgies. I like my sex to be one on one."

"God, but you are making me want that 'one on one' right now"—Edward licked Alex's lush lower lip—"but we can't do it here in the hallway."

"True, the neighbors might complain. Still want that drink?"

"Not as much as I want you."

"Good boy." Alex patted Edward's butt. "But I have to confess to being starving hungry. I didn't have time for lunch, so if you don't mind, we could stop for a quick bite on the way to my place, which is, I think you'll agree, where we want to be. Yes?"

"You'll get no argument from me, sir, especially as you're going to be out of town for the next few days, and I already know I'm gonna miss you like heck."

After kissing him again, Alex murmured, "Let's go then." He put his lips to Edward's ear and growled, "I can hardly wait to fuck you again."

"And again, you won't get any argument from me, sir."

Laughing together, they left the apartment building hand in hand and headed for Alex's car.

* * * *

They stopped at a small pizza parlor of Alex's choice where the pies were made to order. While they waited they had a glass of wine and sat at a table near the window. Their conversation in the car had been mostly small talk but not at all stilted, although Edward found himself still a bit distracted by Troy's behavior. He had to remind himself that he didn't really know either of his roommates very well, but if this was typical of Troy, he had no wish to get closer to the guy. However, he didn't want to dwell on Troy's rudeness while he was with Alex. He'd wait until he and Troy were alone before he confronted him.

"So you were so busy today you didn't have time for lunch?" he remarked, after sipping his wine.

"We had a bit of a problem with one of our stellar clients," Alex told him, grimacing. "She's really popular, but she's been getting some bad press recently and wanted Scott, my boss, to fix it. Unfortunately, she's been running around with a pretty scary crowd, and last month she made a fool of herself on *Oprah*, showing up for the interview stoned. You don't do that stuff if you want Oprah to help you regain some of your credibility. Anyway, today she was yelling and threatening and being so obnoxious Scott told her if she didn't cool down, he was no longer going to represent her. She hit the roof and started breaking things. Scott called the building's security and she smacked one of the guys who answered. Before we could stop him, he pepper-sprayed her, and oh my God, if it had been anywhere else but our office, the ruckus that followed would no doubt be all over the tabloid press and TV."

"Wow." Edward gaped at him. "Who was this?"

"Uh...well..." Alex gave him a rueful smile. "I hope you don't mind, but I really shouldn't mention her name. Like I said we're trying to keep it all hush-hush."

"That's okay. I don't follow celebrity news very much."

"Happens to be part of my job." Alex grinned. "Anyway, I took her into my office, got her some eyewash and let her vent, and by the time she'd calmed down, lunch was out of the question. She was worried about getting even more bad publicity if this latest escapade hit the media, but I assured her no one associated with Scott Malone's would leak the story to the press."

"That was nice of you. Do you know her personally?"

Alex nodded. "She was married to a—a friend of mine for a couple of years. It ended badly, and she, uh, well, she isn't really over it yet."

Edward noted the hesitation in Alex's reply, and from his faintly sad expression guessed there was more he wasn't about to disclose just then. Edward felt it best not to ask any leading questions at that moment. Instead, he continued lightly, "Is this pretty standard stuff in your line of work?"

Alex chuckled. "Not really, but when you're dealing with over-inflated egos on one hand and panicky low self-esteem on the other, it can get, shall we say, interesting. The good thing is, I avoided a complaint being filed and she and Scott made up, so that was a load off my mind."

"I bet."

"She has a movie in production and will be in Vancouver for a couple of weeks, so maybe the fact she'll have to concentrate on her role, which I understand could be Oscar material, will help her get over her depression." He looked up as their pizzas were set in front of them. "Mmm, smells delicious."

"The best in town," the waiter told them. "Enjoy."

They both dug in and the waiter was right, Edward thought, they could very well be the best in town.

Alex smiled, enjoying the obvious relish with which Edward started to devour his pizza. The night they'd spent together revealed to Alex that Edward had an engaging, shy appeal, but there was an undercurrent of feistiness that told Alex he was no pushover. He might need that particular asset when dealing with his roommates—especially Troy.

He'd been looking forward to their date all day. It was just a pity Lena had shown up at the office. She always brought with her a host of memories of times past, always wanting to talk about Hank, although that hadn't been uppermost in her mind today after the security guard had pepper-sprayed her. Her language had been choice but at least Scott had taken back his threat to stop representing her. Alex had been friends with Lena Miles for a long time, and he really liked her, loved her really, despite her propensity to cause havoc when she was upset. Hank had been good at calming her, and now it seemed it was up to him to take over.

"Are you okay?"

Edward's concerned voice broke into his thoughts, and he was glad of it. It didn't do to dwell too much on things he couldn't change.

"Yes, I'm fine," he replied.

"Oh good, you went kinda quiet there," Edward said, then added slyly, "I thought maybe you were reconsidering Troy's offer."

"No way!" Alex shook his head adamantly. "And it worries me that you share an apartment with a guy who's obviously a bit of a flake. Is your other roommate his partner?"

"No, I think they've known each other for some time, but they're not a couple. I have to admit, I really don't know that much about either of them. We hardly see one another as a matter of fact."

"Maybe that's a good thing," Alex remarked. "Not a good idea to get close to someone who's so open about his drug use. I just hope he doesn't deal too." He gestured at their plates that still had half their pizzas on them. "What say we get these boxed and finish them later at my place?" He lowered his voice a little. "I have an urge to kiss you again and it might get me banned from coming back here."

Edward chuckled. "Can't have you banned from having *the best pizza in town*."

"No, please. Anything but that!" Alex took their plates over to the counter and asked the server to box the pizzas. "You can put them in the same box," he told the young man, then thought maybe Edward would object to having his half-eaten pizza in the same box with the one Alex had been chewing on. "Is that okay?"

"Sure," Edward said. Once outside he added, "Considering what we've been doing with our mouths since we met, I don't think mixing our pizzas will hurt us."

Alex laughed and put an arm round Edward's shoulders. "You're right, and when we get back to my place, I have some other things I want to do with our mouths, and they don't involve pizza."

"Sounds good to me."

* * * *

"So, Ellingsworth…" Alex glanced at Edward as he drove them to his house. "I looked it up on the map."

"You did?" Edward turned a look of amazement on Alex. "Why?"

"Because I was curious as to where it actually was. Knowing you came from there and seemed pretty happy about it — leaving it, I mean."

"You have no idea."

"You have family there?"

"Oh yes, mother, father and brother — all well and probably doing better than ever now that they don't have me as a constant reminder their youngest son is going to hell."

"Did they really say that?" Alex tried to sound more concerned than appalled. Obviously it wasn't a surprising news bulletin. He might have come from a more accepting family but Edward's situation was far from unique. "I've never quite been able to understand that mentality," he added quietly.

"It's still fairly common." Edward's tone was matter-of-fact. "My folks didn't throw me out but they made my life pretty miserable — especially my brother. God, when I think of how much he must have hated me to have done the things he did. I mean, there was never any love lost between us. Craig's a born bully, but —" He stopped talking and slumped back against the car seat's headrest.

"I'm so sorry." Alex placed his hand on Edward's thigh and gave it a gentle squeeze.

"Listen to me, putting a giant damper on the evening—but you did ask." Edward sounded as if he was trying to chuckle but he didn't quite make it.

Alex squeezed Edward's thigh again, his gentleness at odds with the anger that coursed through him on hearing what Edward had been subjected to by his own family. "How old is your brother?" he asked keeping his voice steady.

"Twenty-six last birthday."

"Old enough to know better."

Edward laughed at that statement. "They're all old enough to know better, don't you think? But they listen to the right-wing extremists and the Bible thumpers, and according to them there's no place in a decent Christian family for the likes of me. And you know something? I tend to agree."

Alex pulled into his driveway and stopped the car. He leaned over and took Edward in his arms, then laid a soft kiss on his lips. "I'm glad you're here with me," he murmured after a moment or two. "I think you need some TLC and I'm the guy who wants to give it to you."

Edward felt the sting of gathering tears in his eyes. He'd never known this kind of intimacy combined with such a warm sense of comfort, but here, wrapped in Alex's arms, he could, for the moment, forget the shit his life at home had become since coming out to his family. Alex was everything he'd always longed for in a companion—kind, considerate, easy to talk to, a great kisser, not to mention hot in bed—but they'd only just met and it was way too soon to be pinning any hopes on a lasting relationship between them. He'd probably scare the man away if he had a clue as to what was spinning through Edward's mind. This was a character flaw of which Edward was only too aware—the tendency to hang his hopes and dreams on someone who showed him affection. He'd made this mistake before, had resolved never to do it again, and here he was, standing on the brink of making the same mistake all over again.

The touch of Alex's lips, his whispered, "Where'd you go?" jerked him out of his jumbled thoughts.

"Sorry, my mind goes off in weird directions sometimes."

Alex kissed him on the cheek then pulled back from their embrace. "Come on, let's go inside. You need cheering up."

They got out of the car and walked the few steps to the front door. As Alex inserted the key into the lock he said, "Just so you know, you can talk to me about whatever's troubling you. I'm a really good listener. Not saying I can solve or take away your problems, but sometimes just getting it off your chest can help."

"Thanks," Edward mumbled following him inside. "But I don't want to cast gloom and doom on our evening. You're leaving tomorrow and I don't want you thinking, 'Thank God I won't have to listen to any more of that guy's whining'."

Alex flipped the switch for the living room lights then turned to face Edward. "You think I'm that shallow? That I regard your obvious distress over what happened between you and your family, and whoever, as simply whining? Okay, we've just met and you don't really know me, but this is how two people get to know each other better—by talking and listening, by sharing."

"But—" Edward tried to interrupt.

"Yeah, I know, I know," Alex continued, "it's probably too soon for us to be getting into deep and life-changing conversations. And, of course," he added with a wry quirk to his lips, "you can always tell me that it's none of my damned business, but I just want you to understand, I'm here to listen if you want to vent."

"You are just...so nice, Alex."

Alex chuckled. "I've heard being thought of as 'nice' can be the death knell to the start of a beautiful friendship." He pulled Edward into his arms. "Besides, how d'you know there's not a scary person lurking under this *nice* exterior?"

Edward grinned weakly. "It wouldn't be the first time I've made that kind of mistake — but I don't think that's the case with you." *At least I hope I'm right about that.*

Alex tightened his arms around Edward and kissed him deep and hard, taking Edward's breath away and seeming to tilt his world on its axis. He felt like he could stand there forever, letting Alex kiss him and kissing him back while their bodies ground together, their erections aligned perfectly for some serious frottage.

"Bed?" Alex murmured when they finally broke off the kiss.

"Yes," Edward replied through swollen lips. Whatever they were going to talk about could wait. *First thing's first...*

* * * *

Alex threw back the comforter and the top sheet. "Gotta get you naked." He slipped his hands under Edward's polo shirt. "Your shirt's a nice color but I like the one underneath better."

"I'm kinda pale, right now," Edward said with a self-conscious laugh.

"You're kinda beautiful," Alex murmured, pulling the polo over Edward's head. He leaned in to nuzzle at Edward's nipples, tonguing and nibbling each one in turn then raining licks and kisses on Edward's chest between the two hard nubs. "And you taste so fucking good too. Your skin is so soft and smooth. Mmm…" He looked up at Edward with a mischievous grin. "Do all Southern gentlemen have skin like silk?"

"What?" Edward sounded even more self-conscious. "Uh… I don't know. Well, not the *gentlemen* I've ever been with."

'Gentlemen' was uttered with more than a hint of bitterness and Alex could have kicked himself for, however inadvertently, bringing Edward an unpleasant memory from the past. Well, he'd work on erasing whatever it was from Edward's mind. He cupped the back of Edward's head then brought him in close for a long and loaded kiss. At the same time he squeezed Edward's left butt cheek with his other hand then slipped a finger into the warm cleft, probing firmly at Edward's hole. Edward responded by moaning softly and pressing his groin against Alex's, sensually rubbing their erections together.

He started to feverishly attack the buttons on Alex's shirt and helped him shrug out of it. Alex threw it to one side then quickly toed off his shoes and stepped out of his pants while Edward dropped his jeans and briefs then kicked them away. Once they were naked, Alex pulled him back into his arms and together they fell across the bed, their mouths locked in yet another long and passionate kiss as they clung to each other. Alex slipped one hand down between their torsos and gripped Edward's erection. Slowly, almost leisurely, he began to pump it, eliciting a groan of pleasure from Edward, his breath sweet on Alex's tongue.

He pulled back a little. "Are you still tender from last night?"

Edward blinked then gave a slight nod. "Just a bit, but if you want to fuck me, that's okay."

"No, Edward, it's not okay. I want you to enjoy my being inside you as much as I do. I don't want you to just grin and bear it. How about we reverse positions this time?"

"You mean...? But I've never —"

"There's a first time for everything and I'd be very happy to be the first guy you fucked." He reached for the lube and condom and handed Edward the lube. "Here, get me ready."

Edward took the tube and found himself getting even more excited at the prospect of being on top. Excited, and very nervous. What if he was clumsy and hurt Alex? He looked up at Alex's defined torso as he straddled Edward's thighs. He laid down the tube and ran his hands over Alex's abs and chest, gently teasing each nipple between his thumb and forefinger.

"Mmm." Alex smiled down at him, his eyes hooded with unconcealed lust. He picked up the lube and coated Edward's fingers then raised his hips and guided Edward's hand into the cleft between his buttocks. Edward pushed into Alex's heat and Alex squirmed over Edward's fingers. "Feels good," he murmured and reached for the condom. After ripping the packet open with his teeth he quickly sheathed Edward's aching erection then positioned himself directly over the throbbing shaft. Edward gasped as Alex sank slowly down, not stopping until he had all of Edward's cock deep inside him.

Edward ran his hands up and down the sides of Alex's torso, marveling at this sensation of complete exhilaration that had overtaken him. Not in his wildest dreams had he ever imagined this happening. This beautiful man riding his cock, his perfect body undulating rhythmically over him, the feel of the smooth, tanned skin under his fingers sending shivers of sheer ecstasy through him. He pushed his hips upward and Alex groaned.

"That's it," he murmured. "Fill me up, Edward, fuck me hard."

Edward pushed up again, meeting Alex's downward thrust, and soon they were matching each other's rhythm, bodies moving in a sensual counterpoint. Alex leaned down and covered Edward's mouth with his, tangling their tongues together in a kiss that robbed Edward of every rational thought and made him drive harder and harder into Alex's core.

Alex reared back, supporting himself with a hand on either side of Edward's thighs. His sweat-soaked torso gleamed in the light from the bedside lamp and the visual of his taut abs straining as he drove himself up and down on Edward's shaft brought Edward to the point of no return. He reached out and gripped Alex's erection, pumping it in time to the motion of their bodies. He gave a cry of satisfaction when a stream of cum erupted from Alex's cock, splattering over Edward's chest and chin. That was all it took. One, two thrusts more and Edward jetted into the condom buried in Alex's heat. Alex collapsed on top of him and held him, crooning indistinguishable words softly in his ear.

* * * *

When Edward opened his eyes, Alex was leaning over him, gently massaging his chest.

"You must be an angel," Edward whispered, "because I know I died and went to heaven a little while ago."

Alex grinned at him. "It was quite beautiful, wasn't it?"

"Beautiful doesn't come close. In just two days you've taught me more about pleasure than I ever thought was possible."

"You are quite welcome," Alex said with a teasing smile.

"Why're you smiling?"

"Because I love listening to the way you talk. Don't ever try to lose your Southern accent. It's very attractive, and very *sexy*." He kissed Edward's lips to emphasize the word. "I don't think I asked you when you moved to LA." He gently pushed back a stray blond lock of hair that had fallen over Edward's forehead.

"Just over a month ago. I answered an ad on an online job site, fixed up an interview and took the chance I'd get the job."

"That eager, huh?"

"You have no idea how much I wanted to get away. I figured if I didn't get that particular job I could do the rounds until I found something. As luck would have it, the bank manager I interviewed with was desperate. He'd lost two tellers in less than a week so he needed me to start straight away. I was happy to oblige." He lifted his head and stole a kiss from Alex. "It's so nice being here with you, Alex."

"The feeling is mutual." Alex ran his hand over Edward's chest, caressing the smooth skin. He sensed

Edward was trying to change the subject but he wanted to stay on track, learn a little more about Edward's past. "Have you...uh, been in touch with your parents since you left? Just to let them know you're okay?"

"Nope. They have my cell number. If they were interested in how I was they could call."

"Edward..."

"Let me explain something so you don't think I'm some jerk who couldn't care less about his family's welfare."

"Whoa, when did I ever give you the impression that thought had even crossed my mind?"

"You haven't—sorry. I didn't mean to imply that at all." Edward sighed. "When I came out to them my father reacted so violently I thought he might just kill me right there and then—or have a freaking heart attack. I'd never seen him behave like that before. He lurched out of his chair so fast it skidded across the dining room floor and crashed against the wall. He screamed at me, words—God, Alex, it's hard to describe how I felt at that moment—words straight out of the Bible—words like sodomite and hellfire punishment—and my mother just sat staring at me, her face so hard and unforgiving, her eyes cold with no love in them for me. Right then, I could see her distancing herself from me. And asshole Craig, my brother, laughing his fool head off. He said he was going to beat the crap out of me."

"Surely your parents wouldn't allow that?"

"They'd have turned a blind eye, but I didn't need their protection, Alex. Over the years I'd learned to take care of myself. When I was a little kid, Craig used me as a punching bag any chance he could get. Mom and Dad didn't even seem to notice, and of course

Craig warned me he'd beat up on me even more if I ever said a word about what he was doing. So in junior high I joined the wrestling team and started working out, went to a class and learned some defensive moves. I was able to get in a couple of punches now and then when he'd start his crap. I managed to take him by surprise once or twice, but then of course he'd get his buddies, mindless morons like himself, to back him up, and I went down a couple of times."

And even that wasn't the worst of it...

"Jeez, why am I telling you all this?" He rolled onto his side to face Alex. "I want this evening to be about you and me. Just you and me, not my folks, not my jerk of a brother who doesn't deserve one moment of thought from me."

Alex held him close. "I hoped it might help if you talk about it. Those kind of memories can be hard to live with if you let them fester."

"What I want are better memories," Edward said. "Moments like this that I can remember with a smile on my face. While you're gone I'll be able to play back in my head everything we've done together. The way your kisses feel, the sensation of having you inside me, of being inside you, your beautiful face..."

"You're quite the romantic, aren't you?" Alex murmured, and kissed Edward's forehead. "I won't forget our two nights together either. They'll have a special place in my memory."

A concerned expression creased Edward's brow. "I will see you again, won't I? I mean when you come back from New York."

Alex smiled. "I want that, and I was hoping you would too."

"You bet I do."

"I get back on Saturday morning, so perhaps we can meet for dinner, or you could come round and I'll prepare something."

"You'll have just got back. Let me take you to dinner, then we can head back here, if that's okay. I'm not ready to have you stay over at my place yet. It needs some work."

"Mmm…" Alex ran his forefinger over Edward's lower lip. "I have to say I'm still not happy about you sharing with someone like Troy. He smells to me of trouble."

Edward sucked Alex's finger into his mouth, teasing it with his tongue before letting it slip out. "Now there's someone else I don't want to talk about right now. Talk about a buzz kill, Alex."

They chuckled together then Alex said, "You're right. Enough talking, more kissing."

"And everything else that follows," Edward whispered.

Chapter Four

Three days later

Edward hadn't quite realized just how much he would miss Alex's company while he was in New York. Business at the bank was slow mid-week, giving him too much time to think about Alex and the incredible nights they'd spent together. Nights he could hardly wait to repeat again and again. Alex had phoned him three times since he'd been gone – long phone calls that had Edward jerking off while listening to his deep, sexy voice. Phone sex would never replace the real thing, but it was gratifying to hear Alex's breathing become labored as he neared orgasm.

He phoned on the Friday night to remind Edward he'd be back in LA Saturday morning.

"As if I'd forget that," Edward said. "I can't wait to see you. Did you get everything taken care of?" Alex had told him one of their clients was unhappy with the agency's recent publicity coverage and he had been given the unenviable task of meeting with the sour celebrity, and smoothing things over.

"Yes, all's well in that particular camp. I got him lined up with a morning TV interview which went very well, and the *New Yorker* is going to run a piece on him next month. I'm calling you early because I have a dinner date with him and his wife which will most likely go on into the wee small hours. Now he's a happy man I can't get him to stop talking!"

After telling Edward he was 'itching' to see him again, Alex hung up. Edward had just turned off his phone when the front door to the apartment was pushed open so violently it crashed against the entryway wall.

"What the — ?"

His roommate, Troy, staggered in, his face deathly pale. Without a word, he headed straight for his room and slammed the door. Kevin followed seconds later, and from his grim expression, was thoroughly pissed off.

"What's going on?" Edward asked.

"He's fucked up. I found him puking outside. I asked him what was wrong and all I got was a garbled bunch of words that made no sense, not even to him I should think, then more puking."

"Should we call nine-one-one? He looks terrible."

"If I know Troy," Kevin said, his face showing his disgust, "he's been mixing his drugs. If he goes to the hospital they'll have to report him for drug use, and believe me he won't thank us for that."

"He's done this before?"

Kevin nodded then grimaced as the sound of retching came from Troy's room. "He does sound worse this time."

"Maybe we should go in there. He might hurt himself."

Kevin sighed. "It won't be pretty and he's not going to appreciate us trying to help. He gets really nasty when he's like this. It might be best to let him sleep it off."

"You think?" Edward frowned as he heard a thud then a moan of distress. "I'm going to see if he's okay." He pushed Troy's bedroom door open and found his roommate sprawled on the floor beside the bed, blood seeping from a gash on his forehead.

"Shit," Kevin muttered behind him. "He must have banged his head on the nightstand."

They both knelt by Troy's unconscious body. "I really think we should call nine-one-one," Edward said. "He could have a concussion. People can die from not having that kind of thing diagnosed right away."

"You're right." Kevin pulled his cell phone from his jacket pocket and hit the emergency number. "He'll just have to suck it up when they find out what's in his blood."

While Kevin reported the accident, Edward got a washcloth from the bathroom to clean up the wound on Troy's head. It was deep and his face had taken on a pale, waxy appearance. *He's going to need stitches.* He remembered reading in some article or other that if you suspect concussion the person should be kept very still. He was glad Troy was showing no signs of coming round, or else he might just try sitting up.

"They'll be here in a few minutes," Kevin said. "How's he doing?"

"Still out, and I don't really know if that's a good thing or not. Did they say what to do in the meantime?"

"Just keep him comfortable. If he regains consciousness we should keep him quiet." He chuckled dryly. "Fat chance of that with Troy."

But Troy didn't wake up and when the paramedics arrived they put him on emergency life support and quickly wheeled him out of the apartment.

"One of you better come with him and prepare to give the doctors some information," a tall, lean young man with a name badge that told them his name was Brad said. "Looks like a drug overdose to me."

"I'll go." Edward and Kevin spoke simultaneously and Edward couldn't help but notice Kevin had his eyes glued on the paramedic's trim body. He rolled his eyes. "We'll both go. You get in the ambulance, Kevin, and I'll follow in my car."

"You sure you're okay to drive?" Brad asked.

"Totally sure," Edward snapped. "Let's go."

* * * *

Several hours later, a thoroughly exhausted Edward returned home. He headed for the kitchen to make himself a cup of green tea to take to his room. Kevin had opted to hang around, waiting for Brad to get off duty. He said he'd sensed an interest from the young paramedic. After several stitches, Troy was going to be okay. They were keeping him overnight for observation, and the doctor had recommended that he see a counselor about his drug use. He added that had his roommates not called for help he might have fallen into a coma and the result would have been much more serious. Troy appeared less than grateful and Kevin informed Edward that the chances of Troy taking the doctor's advice were approximately zero.

Never mind the fact he got lucky the doctor didn't report the incident to the cops.

"He's been doing this stuff for the past several months," Kevin said. "I've tried talking to him but he just tells me to mind my own fuckin' business, so don't even try going there. I've known him for years and he won't listen to me. With someone he barely knows – and by the way," Kevin's voice held a trace of warning as he continued, "has a boyfriend he'd love to get his hands on – he's not likely to listen to you."

Boyfriend. Edward wondered how Alex would react to being called his boyfriend. They'd only been out together twice. Edward was unsure when you could start calling someone your boyfriend. He'd never had one, so the occasion hadn't come up before. Two years ago he'd met a guy online he had thought he could fall for, but that was before their less than stellar night together.

Stan had been so far in the closet he was used to the dark. "I want to have sex with you," he'd confessed one night after they'd been to the movies together, "but I've never done it with anyone I know. Just truck stops and back alley stuff in Charleston. You know, that kind of thing."

Edward knew about 'that kind of thing' but not from personal experience. He wasn't being prudish about it, it had just never appealed to him. He didn't want sex to be a hit-and-run affair. He wanted a relationship. Nevertheless, he let Stan make a move on him in his car after they'd driven so far out of Ellingsworth, Edward was convinced they'd crossed two state lines.

Stan didn't want to kiss, he just wanted to trade blow jobs. Problem was Stan couldn't get hard no matter how long Edward sucked and played with his dick. Edward was hard as a rock, something that seemed to upset Stan to no end. Finally he pulled away and muttered something about it being easier at the truck stops. Edward had tried coaxing him into just holding one another, but Stan didn't want any of that. 'Too girly,' he'd said sneering, and started the car, driving Edward to his parents' house without another word.

Edward had tried phoning the next day and the next, but Stan was 'not at home', and when they had met by accident—an easy occurrence in a small town like Ellingsworth—he'd averted his gaze, pretending not to see Edward.

He gave himself a shake to clear his head. He'd told Alex he didn't want to live in the past, only the new life LA presented. So, why now had he started to remember this? Especially as those memories held no fondness, only reminding him of how desolate his life had been back home. Stan had not been his only bad experience—there had been worse, much worse. It would be great to call Alex his boyfriend, or, even better, his lover—but that was being way too optimistic.

Two nights together does not a relationship make, he told himself.

Hearing the sound of voices in the living room, he thought he'd better make his presence known. "Hey, guys," he said, opening one of the café doors that screened off the kitchen.

"Oh hi, thought you'd be in bed," Kevin replied, pausing in his attempt to dislocate Brad's tonsils with his tongue.

"Just on my way." Edward carried his cup of green tea toward his bedroom. "Don't mind me." It was obvious they weren't about to mind him. Shirts were being removed before Edward could even close his bedroom door. Once inside, he undressed, threw himself down on top of his bed and plugged in his iPad recording of *Adele Live at the Royal Albert Hall.* Adjusting his ear bud, he thought, *Adele should be enough to drown out the noise they're bound to be making any minute now.*

* * * *

Alex relaxed into his aisle seat on the plane back to Los Angeles. He'd opted to take an earlier morning flight as his business with his petulant client had been satisfactorily taken care of. *Celebrities*, he thought wryly. *Wouldn't want to live with one for all the tea in China.* He'd been around them long enough to know that although some were decent, hard-working men and women, there was almost always the need for ego stroking, even among the more established stars. They could get downright prickly sometimes if they felt they weren't getting the kind of attention their stardom merited. But he was used to it, and over the years had managed to maneuver his way around the minefields of short tempers and flaring indignation that were all part and parcel of his job.

One day I might write a book about the more hilarious aspects of dealing with the stars…

Maybe that's why he'd found being with Edward so refreshing. There wasn't any artifice in that young man, as far as he could tell anyway. He considered himself a pretty good judge of character—had to be in his field—and so far Edward just came across as one of the good guys. A bit introverted perhaps, and obviously carrying a lot of hurt and regret from his past, but with some TLC that could be repaired.

His self-esteem could use a bit of a boost without a doubt, and maybe I could be of help there.

His thoughts were interrupted when the man sitting next to him snorted then grumbled, "Breaking news? There's war and famine all over the world and this stupid channel is more interested in some movie star getting herself pepper-sprayed by a security guard."

What?

The man's eyes were riveted on the small screen in front of him. "What program is that?" Alex asked, keeping the tone of his voice on an even keel.

"AMZ or something. Crappy channel, but it's all I can get at the moment. Wish my iPad wasn't busted."

Alex turned on his headset and listened while a blonde woman recounted what had taken place in his office a few days ago.

"Our inside sources tell us that Lena Miles had been making a nuisance of herself and had to be restrained. When she started kicking the security guard he pepper-sprayed her. No charges have been filed but our source says Miss Miles was so furious she threw a tantrum and tried to break things in the office, the one that handles her publicity. Not such a clever idea, huh? Sounds like things are not going well for her ever since her husband, Hank Bartell, died of a drug overdose a year ago. You may remember —"

Damn it! Alex pulled off his headset and sank back in his seat. Who the hell in the office had blabbed that story? He didn't want to hear the account of Hank's death repeated yet again. He remembered that horrendous time all too well and the thought of it even now brought a welling of tears to his eyes. Try as he might to stem the rush of memories, they flooded his mind with a sickening clarity — the hysterical call from Lena in the middle of the night, the nightmare drive to Beverly Hills with Lena calling him every two minutes wanting to know when he'd get there, her refusal to call nine-one-one. "He's still breathing, Alex, he's going to be all right." He'd called the paramedics himself and had let out a sigh of relief when he'd seen the ambulance already at the gates to Hank's mansion. Only, they had been having a problem trying to gain entrance.

"Lena," he'd growled in frustration at her stubbornness. Using the code he had known by heart, he'd signaled for the medics to go on through ahead of him as the gates swung open. By the time he'd reached the house all he'd been able to do was try to calm Lena down while the medic team had attended to Hank. But it was too late. Hank had died there on the bedroom floor despite all attempts to save him. If only Lena had called Emergency when she'd first found him lying in his own vomit, if only he'd been more in Hank's face about his drug use, if only he'd never let Hank go along with the sham marriage just to appease the studios and stave off the early rumors of his homosexuality. Why the hell hadn't he demanded that Hank say *fuck you* to the studio bosses and stay with him. If only he'd fought harder... If only...

He swallowed the sob that had risen dangerously close to escaping his throat, but he could not stop the tears stinging his eyes. *Hank...* So fucking gorgeous with that mane of blond hair and eyes the color of the ocean, such a deep, dark blue. A god among men was the way he'd been described in *People* magazine when they'd named him Sexiest Man Alive.

Alex had agreed. He'd been so in love with him and had enjoyed the silly, secret pride of knowing that he alone knew the real Hank Bartell. Not just the one pictured in the glossy magazines, but the real flesh and blood man with the wicked sense of humor and the tendency to let slip a loud fart now and then. How they had laughed on their first night together when after a bout of mind-blowing sex, they'd lain exhausted in each other's arms. Alex had been just about to drop off to sleep when a colossal fart had sounded from under the sheets.

He'd looked at Hank with wide eyes. "Oops, sorry," Hank had muttered. Alex had giggled as he'd tried to prevent Hank from lifting the sheets. "No, no," he'd yelped. "We'll be gassed by noxious fumes." They'd wrestled amongst the bedding, laughing hysterically like schoolboys.

Hank hadn't been a god, just a man—a gorgeous man, a sweet and gentle man until the drugs had changed him. But not just the drugs. The major change had come after he was told to dump Alex, never see him again, get married, or there would be no guarantee his career would survive. The studio heads had cited several gay scandals that had jeopardized the careers of some of Hollywood's biggest names until they had threatened to sue—or got married. They had already created the myth that Hank and Lena Miles were an item and that 'wedding bells' were definitely in the couple's futures. All Hank and Alex had to do was promise they would not continue their relationship, not even discreetly.

"The paparazzi are everywhere," one of the studio bosses had told Hank. "They're already suspicious. You've just been lucky you and your fella haven't been caught with your pants down. Marrying Lena is the best thing you can do..." Hank's protests had fallen on deaf ears, and Alex had told him he wouldn't forgive himself if Hank's career was soured because of their relationship.

Alex's chest tightened when he remembered their last night together—the tears, the declarations of love, Hank's sudden decision to tell them all to go to hell. He'd take his chances if he was outed.

As much as it had killed him to do it, Alex had dissuaded him from that decision. He knew what the outcome would have been. He'd seen it happen to other stars. Some had found success appearing on the stage or in indie movies—but the truth was, Hank wasn't the greatest actor in Hollywood. His star appeal depended on his amazing looks and his manliness. Alex had loved Hank with all his heart and soul, but he couldn't see him on the Broadway stage reciting lines with conviction. No, Hank belonged on the big screen, where the camera loved him. He was at his best trading punches with criminals, leaping off moving trains or tracking down terrorists. His reputation as the 'sexiest man alive' as he wooed and seduced Hollywood's most beautiful female stars had to endure.

If only it had…

Chapter Five

Saturday morning

Edward opened his eyes and glanced at the digital clock by his bed. "Only seven," he mumbled, "and it's Saturday, no work today." He closed his eyes again, willing himself back to sleep, then he remembered. *Alex gets back today from New York.* The thought made his heart quicken and his cock jump. *Oh, yeah...* He could hardly wait to feel those strong arms around him, that muscular body pressed to his. He was really hard now. He gripped his erection and slid it through his hand. Wait, should he save this for later when he was with Alex? He pondered this for a moment or two. *Nah, I'm young. There's plenty more where this comes from.*

He was about to give in to his carnal desire when he heard Kevin's voice coming from the living room, loud and sounding pissed off. "Okay, asshole, keep your fuckin' hair on. We'll be there as soon as we can." This was followed by a string of expletives then,

"Hey, Ed! Troy needs picking up at the hospital. I'm outta gas so we'll have to use your car."

Cursing, Edward pulled on a T-shirt and shorts then stumbled to the door. "They're releasing him this early?"

"Of course not." Kevin's bed head and the shadows under his eyes told Edward his roomie hadn't had much sleep. "The asshole snuck out. He's waiting for us on the steps outside the hospital."

Edward groaned. "Great. Where's Brad? Couldn't he take you?"

"He left. Said he had first shift or something."

"Okay, let me get my shoes on and grab my car keys."

A few minutes later they were in Edward's car heading for the hospital. Kevin smelled of sex. Edward imagined he still had dried cum, either his or Brad's, on his skin. Not a thought he particularly wanted to entertain.

"How'd he sound?" Edward asked.

"Moronic, as usual," Kevin replied shortly, staring out of the passenger window. "If he keeps this up I'm going to look for a new apartment. You up for a change of scenery? We could get a place together."

"I-I don't know." Edward was surprised by the suggestion.

"Well, you can hang out with Troy if you like, but I tell you it's only going to get worse."

"Not if he gets help."

"He doesn't *want* help." Kevin glared at him. "He snuck out of the hospital so he can go to some party tonight with a bunch of drugged-out losers."

"Jesus…" Edward remembered Alex telling him Troy had invited him to the party—and Troy still intended on going? "We have to stop him," he said firmly.

Kevin snorted with derision. "Good luck with that. He won't listen to anything we have to say."

"What if we lock him in his room?"

"Are you serious?" Kevin laughed out loud. "He'd bust the fucking door down. Honestly, I don't know how we're going to deal with him after this weekend."

Edward's stomach felt suddenly queasy. He hoped like hell Alex would ask him to stay over so he wouldn't have to face the aftermath of Troy's drug bash.

* * * *

Troy looked like hell. His dark hair stuck out in all directions and his complexion lacked any color whatsoever. "What took you so long?" was his grouchy greeting when Edward pulled up outside the hospital. He flung himself inside the back of the car and lay down on the seat.

"Dude, you're in bad shape," Kevin told him. "You sure leaving the hospital is a good idea?"

"I'll feel better later," Troy muttered.

Kevin glanced at Edward. "Sure you will."

"Maybe a long rest in bed would help." Edward glanced at Troy's sallow complexion in his rearview mirror.

"I might take a nap. You don't get a fuckin' minute's sleep in those places." Troy groused. "There's always somebody coming around, making noise, taking blood, adjusting this, that and the other thing. Jesus, how does anybody ever get better in a place like that hellhole? A nap sounds good," he added through a gigantic yawn, "then I gotta get ready for the party tonight. I wouldn't miss out on that for — for free tickets to a Lady Gaga concert!"

Kevin chuckled but Edward shook his head sadly. "Troy, honestly, you shouldn't be going to a party in the shape you're in."

Troy sat up and glared at Edward through the mirror. "What are you, my mother? I don't need you gettin' in my fuckin' business."

"Told ya," Kevin muttered.

"Excuse me for being concerned," Edward said quietly. "I'll make sure it won't happen again."

"Right, but I need one of you to drive me over there tonight."

Edward couldn't believe his ears. The nerve of some guys.

"Well, it won't be me," Kevin said immediately. "Ed's right, you shouldn't even be thinking of going to that stupid party. Besides, I have other plans."

The drive back to the apartment in the heavy silence that ensued seemed to Edward to be endless. All he could hope for at that moment was that he'd soon hear from Alex and he could put all this mess behind him for a few, or, better still, *several* hours — the whole weekend if he got lucky.

After Edward parked the car, Troy flung himself off the back seat, not bothering to say even a muttered 'thanks', just headed up the steps to the front entrance of the building without waiting for either of them. Kevin glanced at Edward and shrugged dismissively.

"I need some coffee," he said, sighing. "Wanna join me at Starbucks?"

Edward nodded and after locking the car he fell in step with Kevin and they walked to the corner coffee shop. "Is it worth even trying to stop him from going to the party tonight?" he asked.

"Nope. This will make the third time he's done this recently."

"But I don't recall him doing this before."

"It's been a month or two since the last one. I honestly didn't think he'd do it again. He was so wasted, a couple of guys dragged him home from wherever they were and left him on the steps outside. He was lucky one of the neighbors coming back from an early morning jog found him, and not the cops. He knocked on the door and told me Troy was outside then he helped me bring him in. Troy spent the whole morning puking his guts up. Probably what saved him, but he doesn't learn. When he was able to get around, he told me what a fantastic time he'd had! Can you believe it?"

"No, I can't. He doesn't ask you to go with him?"

"Once, but I said no way. I don't mind a little weed now and then, but these guys are into the hardcore stuff. Scares me to death."

"Maybe we should stage an intervention."

Kevin stared at him as if he'd grown an extra head. "You have a death wish or something?" He slowed his steps as they approached the coffee shop. "Listen to me, the best thing we can do is let him realize just what he's doing to himself. He will eventually. It might mean he ends up in court, promising to enter rehab, and that's probably the best thing that could happen."

"But what if it kills him before that happens?"

"It won't. Troy is too mean to die."

"Kevin, that's pretty callous. I thought you guys were friends."

Kevin shrugged and pushed the coffee shop door open. "When you've been around him for as long as I have, you start to rethink the meaning of the word 'friend'."

No one was waiting at the counter so they placed their orders right away, Kevin asking for the strongest coffee they had. "Haven't really woken up yet," he muttered, trying to find an empty table. "There's one by the window." He strode off while Edward placed his order for breakfast tea.

Kevin looked up as Edward joined him at the table. "So, you and me... We haven't really had much of a chance to talk apart from discussing Troy's weaknesses."

"No, I guess we haven't. Are you serious about finding another apartment?"

"Probably. I'll wait and see what happens tomorrow."

"What do you expect to happen?"

"Well, either Troy will die of an overdose, or in a fiery car crash, or he'll get arrested. Or he'll have enough sense to stay the night where the party's being held and none of those things will happen. This time."

"Does he have any other close friends apart from you?" Edward asked.

Kevin shrugged then rose to pick up their orders when their names were called. Edward sank back against the hard rungs of the seat and wondered what his next move should be. Alex had been right about this not being the best place for him to live, but he'd considered himself lucky to find the apartment so quickly. He really didn't think moving to another with Kevin was the greatest idea either.

"So..." Kevin was back and placed Edward's cup of tea in front of him. "Tell me about this hunky boyfriend of yours," he said as he took his seat. "What's he do?"

"Uh, he works for a publicity agency."

"Oh yeah?" He took a giant gulp of his coffee. "Which one?"

"I'm not sure." He actually couldn't remember the name of the agency. He'd been too caught up in other aspects of Alex when they'd talked briefly about their respective jobs.

"You think he's the one?"

Edward choked out a laugh. "The one? We've only been on a couple of dates and he's been gone practically all week."

"Yeah, but Troy said he could tell the guy was really into you. He also said he couldn't understand it, but I can see it. You're a cute guy, Edward."

"Uh, thanks. What about you, Kevin?" he asked, hoping he was being subtle enough in veering the conversation away from himself and Alex. "Are you dating anyone right now?"

"Why, wanna apply for the job?" He followed this up with a raucous laugh that had some heads turning their way. "Just kidding. No. Brad, the medic, was just a one-nighter. As a matter of fact, I just ditched the last guy I was dating."

Edward took a sip of his hot tea before asking, "What went wrong?"

"Oh, the usual. He was good-looking but too clingy. I can't stand it when a guy gets hung up on the lovey-dovey stuff and wants more and more of me."

Edward was beginning to wonder just which one of his two roomies was the bigger jerk. "Yeah, that can be awkward all right," he murmured.

Kevin didn't seem to notice the sarcasm in Edward's tone. "And then there was his dick, which was just incredible...ly small." More laughter.

Edward gritted his teeth. "I think we should take these back to the apartment," he said, picking up his container of tea. "I'm feeling a bit bushed."

"Yeah, me too. Let's go."

Offering up a silent prayer of thanks, Edward followed him out of the door.

* * * *

When they got back to the apartment, Troy's bedroom door was closed and they could hear the sound of snoring.

"Good," Kevin said. "And seeing as how he's out of it, that's also what I'm going to do. See ya."

Edward headed for his own room, deciding to take the longest shower of his life. Standing under the hot spray, he wondered when he'd hear from Alex. Perhaps he should call him, or would that appear too needy? Maybe Alex would like to know he was looking forward to seeing him again—after all they had almost made a date for when he got back to LA, hadn't they? He took his time shampooing and conditioning his hair, then using a new body wash he'd picked up the day before. Its fresh pine scent was invigorating, and by the time he rinsed off and stepped out of the shower, he felt more able to face the day. It was just after nine. Too early to call Alex? He could leave a message on his voicemail if he didn't answer.

He picked up his cell and punched in Alex's number. Alex answered after the first ring.

"Hi, it's Edward. I—"

"Hi, Edward. Sorry, I'm at the office. I'll have to call you back." He sounded rushed, even a little distant.

"Oh, okay. I'd thought you'd take the day off."

"I have some damage control to take care of. I'll call you later, okay? Gotta go, bye."

"B—" The sound of disconnect startled him. He stared at his cell for a few seconds, more than a little perturbed by Alex's gruffness. *He must be really upset about something. Damage control. Guess that could mean just about anything.*

Alex put his cell phone aside and bit his lip. He hadn't meant to sound quite so abrupt, but Edward had caught him in the middle of a meeting with Scott, his boss, and Lena's agent, Jeff Harding. Both men were pissed as hell about the TV report on Lena's meltdown of a few days ago.

"I want to know who leaked that story," Jeff said through gritted teeth while glaring at Alex. "And I want the son-of-a-bitch fired, got that? Lena doesn't need this kind of publicity when she's starting a new movie. She's nervous enough as it is, you know how she gets. Some asshole reporters are gonna try to get to her and start asking her about it and I can't be there all the time to shield her from them." He jabbed a finger in Alex's direction. "That's gonna be your job until this dies down."

"Isn't Sophia there with her?" Alex asked.

"Sophia's there, but she's only a goddamn secretary. I want you there to fend off the paparazzi and all those other assholes who'll be on her like a locust swarm."

Scott threw his hands up in protest. "Sophia's more than Lena's secretary. They've been friends for a long time, and Alex isn't a goddamn bodyguard, Jeff. I need him here in the office. He just got back from New York, as you know, and you want him to spend time on location with Lena until the movie's in the can? I don't think so."

"It's only a couple of weeks outta town," Jeff said, "then they'll be back in LA for the final scenes. You guys owe me this for the mess that went on here in this office."

"It's okay, Scott." Alex fingered his cell phone as he spoke, his mind still on how he must have sounded to Edward. He needed to call him back as soon as possible to apologize. "I can take care of Lena for a bit. Where's the location?"

"Vancouver," Jeff told him. "And you need to take the next plane up there. I already texted her to let her know you'll be there this afternoon."

Shit! He wouldn't be able to see Edward before he left. *I need to pack and get to the airport. Damn it, there won't be enough time.*

"This afternoon?" Scott was venting like Alex would love to, but he had to remain cool. Jeff could be the bitch from hell when he wanted to be and if Alex didn't take care of his number one client, Scott's prestige would suffer. The way Scott suddenly shut up told Alex the same thought had just occurred to him.

"Guess I better hit the road," he said, getting to his feet.

"I'll have the ticket waiting for you at the Air Canada desk. The plane leaves at one. Don't miss it. " Jeff looked smug. He liked to get his way.

"First class I hope." Alex was kidding but Jeff's snort of derision made his hackles rise anyway. *Cheap bastard.*

"She's at the Concordia Hotel," Jeff said. I'll call in a reservation for you, on the same floor if I can arrange it."

"Okay, boss." Alex looked at Scott's unhappy expression. "See you in a couple of weeks. You can email me any stuff you need me to take care of."

On the way out of the building, he punched in Edward's number. "Hey," he said when Edward answered. "Sorry about earlier. I was in a meeting."

"That's okay, I was just surprised you were back at work so soon. Are we still on for this evening?"

"'Fraid not. I have to go to Vancouver this afternoon."

"Oh…"

Edward's disappointment was clear enough in that one word. "Yeah, I'm upset too. This came out of the blue, but I have to go take care of an important client. I'll be gone about two weeks."

"That long?" There was a moment of silence then Edward asked, "D'you have time for lunch or a coffee or something?"

"No, I'm really sorry, Edward. My plane leaves at one and I haven't even had time to pack yet."

"I could drive you to the airport if you like?"

Alex hesitated. It seemed like a bit of an imposition when he could just as easily call for a cab, but Edward seemed eager enough to do it, and it would be nice to have his company on what could sometimes be a slog of a drive through heavy traffic.

"You don't mind?" he asked finally.

"Of course not. At least we'll be able to say goodbye properly. I'll pick you up at your place in, say, an hour?"

"That'd be perfect. Thanks, Edward."

"My pleasure. I might even get a goodbye kiss out of it?"

"You can count on it."

Alex closed his phone, smiling. He'd been looking forward to seeing Edward when he got back and the morning meeting had come as a bit of a shock. No way had he anticipated being packed off to Vancouver on the same day he returned from New York. The only sleep he'd managed had been on the plane, Scott's summons to the office coming as Alex had arrived at LAX—and here he was about to head back there in an hour or so. Who said working for a star agency was glamorous?

Edward's sigh as he closed his phone was one of both despondency and yet excitement as he got ready to drive to Alex's house. He'd see him in about an hour, but then he was going to be gone for two weeks. Damn, but he'd been anticipating spending the evening with Alex so much, having dinner together, gazing into those amazing dark eyes, feeling the softness of his lips...

"Okay, that's enough," he said aloud, startling himself by the vehemence in his voice. "No point in torturing yourself." *And if in two weeks when he gets back and maybe still wants to see me, we can make it another night to remember. I can deal with that.*

In the meantime he just had to put up with Troy's drug episodes and Kevin's snarkiness. *Maybe it's time I look for a place by myself.*

* * * *

He left the apartment a little earlier than he needed to in the hope that he'd find Alex still inside his house and maybe coerce him into a quickie blow job. Chuckling to himself at his unusual audacity, he stepped on the gas but was quickly disillusioned by the amount of Saturday morning traffic all seeming to go in his direction. By the time he reached Alex's street, he could see him standing outside his house and glancing at his watch.

Well, that's just fucking fantastic, he groused, pulling up in front of Alex's driveway and braking harder than he had to. "Sorry." He jumped out of the car to open the trunk. "Traffic was a bitch."

"Don't worry." Alex gave him a quick kiss on the cheek. "I know a shortcut to the freeway." They loaded Alex's two bags into the trunk then set off, Edward following Alex's directions to the 405 freeway.

"I really appreciate this, Edward." Alex stroked Edward's thigh as he spoke, sending shivers all through him.

"I can pick you up when you get back if you like." Edward shifted in his seat to ease his growing hard-on.

"Are you sure?"

"Totally sure." He glanced at him quickly. "Let me just put this out there. I've missed you the whole time you've been gone, and I'll miss you even more this time. I hope that doesn't make me sound needy and make you feel uncomfortable or anything."

"No, it doesn't. I'm glad you feel that way, because I've missed you too, Edward, and to say I'm pissed about these unexpected events is putting it mildly." He explained what had been discussed at the meeting, and why he had to leave at such short notice. "You'll most likely see it on TV so I'm not letting the cat out of the bag when I tell you it's the agency's client, Lena Miles, I'm going to Vancouver to see.

"Lena has a very fragile psyche at the best of times and if reporters start bugging her while she's trying to work, she's likely to have another meltdown and cost the producers a ton of money by missing days of shooting. So, I'll be there to fend off the pests and keep her occupied with positive stuff."

He took Edward's free hand in his. "When I get back I'll tell you more of the history between Lena and myself. So, what have you been up to since I've been gone?"

Edward squeezed Alex's fingers. "Nothing much until last night when Troy came home stoned out of his mind and Kevin and I had to take him to Emergency."

Alex grimaced. "I was afraid of something like that happening."

"It gets worse. He called this morning yelling that he'd snuck out of the hospital and wanted us to come pick him up right away. All because he wants to go some party tonight—the one he told you about, remember? We tried to talk him out of it, but he told us to mind our own fuckin' business. So I guess he's going, and honestly, Alex, I don't want to be there when and if he gets home from wherever he's going. Kevin's talking about getting a new place and asked me if I'd go with him, but here's the other thing—he's a bit of a jerk too. I'm seriously thinking of finding my own place."

"Well, in the meantime..." Alex dug in his pants pocket and pulled out a key. "After you drop me off, go back to my house and spend the night there."

"Oh, I can't impose on you like that, Alex."

"Yes, you can, and it's not an imposition." He pushed the key into Edward's hand. "It's a spare. There's some food in the fridge, some beer too, I think. Call the apartment tomorrow and if things are okay and you want to go back, fair enough, but if there's chaos, stay at my place until things have calmed down. We'll talk more about this when I get back, okay?"

"Alex..."

"Listen, I haven't been happy about you sharing with Troy since the night he told me about this damn party. The guy's a drug addict and by association with him you could be dragged into something really bad. The fact he snuck out of the hospital might just be enough for the doctors to report his using to the authorities. You don't want to be caught up in any drug related problems, believe me. Now, you'll use the key, please?"

"I can't believe how nice you're being to me. You hardly know me."

"I know enough to care about you, Edward."

His hand was on Edward's thigh again and Edward felt himself grow harder than before. "God, but I wish you weren't leaving."

"The feeling's mutual," Alex murmured.

* * * *

When they arrived at the airport Alex said, "Pull into the section marked One Hour Waiting Only. We've made good time so I have a few minutes before I have to check in."

As Edward pulled into an empty bay the overhead light blinked out. "Wow, that's handy. I can kiss you without anyone seeing."

"Not handy." Alex pushed himself nearer Edward and gazed into his eyes. "Magic..."

For a moment Edward almost believed him. *Hell, I'll believe anything this guy tells me when he looks at me like that*. Instead of speaking, he parted his lips and took

Alex's kiss eagerly. Their arms wrapped around each other in the confined space, their bodies straining in an effort to get as close as they could. Alex slid his hands under Edward's T-shirt, and stroked Edward's nipples with his thumbs. He leaned in to lick and nibble on them then went lower, his hot kisses leaving an unbearably erotic trail over Edward's fevered flesh.

He was so hard he thought he'd come right then and there in his briefs, a feeling that spiraled in intensity as Alex unbuttoned his jeans and released his aching erection.

"Jesus..." Edward gasped when Alex took the head of his cock into his mouth, tonguing the slit, bringing Edward to the edge of orgasm. *Oh, God, maybe I should've jerked off this morning after all.* Alex cupped Edward's balls, squeezing gently while his lips glided down then back up the length of Edward's pulsing shaft.

"Alex, stop, I'm *coming.*"

Alex made a muffled noise that sound vaguely like 'good' and sucked harder. Edward's climax exploded out of him, leaving him limp and gasping for air. The car's interior suddenly felt unbearably warm. Alex held him until he softened then looked up at Edward with that wicked gleam in his eyes Edward was beginning to know quite well.

"How was that?" he asked, tucking Edward's cock back into his briefs.

"Unbelievable."

"That's what I hoped you'd say." He glanced at his watch. "Gotta go." He leaned over and kissed Edward, sliding his tongue into Edward's mouth, letting him taste himself. When he pulled back he smiled. "Waiting two weeks for you to return the favor is going to be a challenge."

Edward flung his arms round Alex's neck and kissed him with such fervor that Alex had to forcibly pry his lips free. "Wow," he said chuckling. "Keep that up and the plane will leave without me. Just save it all for when I get back."

"Call me when you get there?"

"I will. Now I really have to go."

Edward helped him with his bags to the elevator. "Better say goodbye here." Edward swore he could see genuine sadness in Alex's expression.

"You hurry back, y'hear?" he whispered, then pressed his lips to Alex's once more.

"Don't forget, stay in my house as long as you have to." Alex stepped into the elevator, and Edward gave him a little wave as the doors slid shut. The next two weeks were going to be a challenge for them both.

Chapter Six

Edward stopped by the apartment on his way back from the airport. Staying over at Alex's house, he needed at least a change of clothing, his toothbrush and comb. Kevin wasn't home when he got there, and it appeared that Troy was still sleeping off his wild night. He packed a small overnight bag, throwing in a clean T-shirt, underwear and socks and his toilet bag. He kept his movements as quiet as possible. The last thing he needed was to wake Troy and have him start asking all over again for a lift to the party tonight. Fortunately, no one was stirring in Troy's room.

Maybe he'll sleep right through and forget all about going out. I can only hope.

* * * *

It seemed strange at first being alone in Alex's house. He wandered from room to room to familiarize himself with the layout and couldn't help but be impressed with the orderliness of things. Nor could he help but compare it to the less than pristine condition of the apartment he shared with Troy and Kevin. He'd seen the state of their bedrooms and realized that just because they were gay didn't make them house proud. Edward figured Alex had someone come in to clean and polish once in a while, if not regularly. With his heavy work schedule it would be hard to maintain the house in this fashion.

In the living room there was a bookcase he hadn't noticed before, but then, on the two occasions he'd been here, he hadn't really been too interested in the furniture. He walked over to see what kind of books might interest Alex, but what immediately took his attention was a photograph of a man on the top shelf. A gorgeous man with a golden tan, a mane of blond hair and eyes of such a dark blue Edward could almost feel the intensity of his gaze. It was autographed, *For Alex, my love always, Hank.*

He looks familiar, but how in hell would I have known someone that good-looking? Maybe he's one of the celebrities Alex represents. That's it, a movie star — and now when he thought about it — *Right, he was voted the world's sexiest man a couple of years ago* — Hank Bartell.

His gaze shifted to the photograph next to the one of the handsome movie star. It was of Alex and Hank with a beautiful woman between them. He recognized her as Lena Miles, the one Alex had told him had caused a ruckus in his office, the one he was going to Vancouver to look after.

Would Hank Bartell be there too?

The surge of jealousy he felt startled him.

You have no right to feel jealous, you've only known him a week. He had a whole lifetime before you met him, and besides you don't know what their relationship was — is?

And there was something else, something he should remember. Right at that moment he wished he paid more attention to celebrity news. He pulled his iPhone from his pocket and went online. He clicked on the Google icon then punched in Hank Bartell's name and gasped when under Hank's image he read the words, Born 1983 — Died 2013.

He sat down on the nearest chair and stared at the screen in shock as he read a reprint of an *LA Times* report of Hank's death.

Hank Bartell, one of Hollywood's busiest stars and twice voted the world's sexiest man alive by People *magazine, died of a drug overdose at his Beverly Hills mansion late last night. Lena Miles, his wife and co-star in Bartell's latest movie, called 9-1-1 after finding her husband on their bedroom floor. Ms. Miles said she had been out with some friends and returned home to find Bartell in distress. She also called a close friend, Alex Martinez, who confirmed to this reporter that Bartell died before the paramedics could transport him to the hospital. Martinez, who was fending off reporters from interviewing Lena Miles, also said that Miss Miles was understandably distraught and any statements would be made through her agent...*

Edward remembered the conversation he'd had with Alex in the pizza parlor on their second night together when Alex had told him Lena had been married to a friend of his. But it hadn't worked out, he'd added. From the fleeting sad expression on Alex's face, Edward had intuited there might be more to the story than Alex had been willing to tell him at that moment. Now he knew why.

God, how terrible to lose a friend that way...

He couldn't help wondering if perhaps there had been more than just friendship between Alex and Hank, but Hank was married to Lena and Alex didn't strike him as the kind of man who would have an affair with a married man. Yet what did he really know about him? Only that he seemed like a sweet and caring person, and one who could take Edward to the stars when they made love.

Sighing, he stood and examined the sound system on one of the shelves—didn't look too complicated. He jabbed at one of the buttons and immediately the room was filled with the sound of soft jazz. A quick look at the row of CDs on another shelf made it clear Alex had an eclectic taste in music. Miles Davis, Ella Fitzgerald and Tony Bennett sat side by side with Cher, Adele and classical collections that included Debussy and Beethoven. The array of books reflected that same varied taste. John Grisham, Diana Gabaldon, Robert Crais were represented along with Ray Bradbury, the poems of Maya Angelou and essays by David Sedaris and Christopher Hitchens. All these made him reflect on the fact that they'd never discussed books or music, or even movies. He smiled wryly, reminding himself that both their evenings together had been all about some pretty torrid sex.

After leaving the living room, he found the kitchen and opened the refrigerator. Alex had said there was some kind of food and he suddenly realized he was famished. He'd had nothing since the tea at Starbucks. In the fridge there were some cold cuts and cheese slices, carefully wrapped. He took them over to the counter and noticed a handwritten note lying there.

Señor Alex, some fixings for sandwiches are in the fridge. There is bread in the pantry. I know you will be hungry after your trip. I hope all went well.
Blanca.

So Alex had someone to look after him, and the house, when he was away. That would account for the pristine condition of the place. He got the bread and some mayo and made a passable sandwich, pouring himself a glass of water to wash it all down. He sat on a counter stool, munching happily, listening to the soothing music being piped in from the console in the living room.

I could get used to this, he thought, looking around, imagining Alex and him coming home from work, having a drink while fixing dinner, talking about their respective days.

Well, isn't this the most ridiculous flight of fancy you've ever had? Almost as stupid as when you believed that asshole Matt, back in Ellingsworth, actually meant what he'd said before you let him fuck you.

Christ, but he so did not want to think about all that now. Hadn't he left all that behind? All the despicable words spewing from a mouth that had earlier been used to kiss his lips and suck his cock—all because Craig, his bullying brother, had found them together in Edward's bedroom. Craig had at first laughed his fool head off, then he'd threatened to tell every single one of Matt's friends he was a fag. Edward had listened, horrified at the betrayal, to the lies that came so easily from Matt. He wasn't a fag. Edward had forced himself on him, tearing his clothes off. He'd been completely taken by surprise and was trying to stop Edward when Craig had barged in and found them together, naked.

Edward had seen that Craig hadn't believed a word of it. After all, Matt's quarterback physique would've ruled out most anyone from overpowering him. But Edward had known his brother loathed him enough that he would pretend to go along with Matt's story, even encouraging Matt to punch Edward — "So he'll never try that crap again" — and Matt had done just that, swinging so hard he'd almost broken Edward's nose. He'd lain there after Matt and Craig had left him alone, and it was then he'd made the decision to leave. There was no point in looking for support from his parents. In their eyes he was tainted, a lost cause destined for hellfire. Craig, despite being a bully and a sexist pig, was their golden boy. They could overlook his uncouth behavior, but they could never condone Edward's 'choices'.

He supposed he should pity Matt for his cowardice and the fact he'd condemned himself to a life of lies and loneliness, but he hadn't yet come that far. The bitter memory of that day and the subsequent humiliation he'd suffered from Craig's never-ending taunting still left a sourness in his stomach when he dwelt on it for too long.

Just like I'm doing now — Stop with the self-pity, for God's sake!

He jumped when his cell phone, sitting on the counter beside him, rang suddenly. He glanced at the caller ID screen. *Alex.* He hadn't expected to hear from him so soon.

"Hi, Alex, is everything okay?"

"Yeah, except I'm in Vancouver, and you're in LA." He chuckled before continuing. "I hope you took me up on the offer to stay over at my place."

"I did, thank you." It was amazing how just the sound of Alex's voice could make him feel so much better than he had a few moments ago. "Uh, how is Lena, your client?"

"Haven't seen her yet. She's up in Whistler on location. I expect her back at the hotel in about an hour. Hey, I was thinking. How would you like to fly up here for a couple of days over the weekend? Maybe you could ask your boss for an extra day or two off."

Edward felt a surge of excitement. Alex was asking him to join him in Vancouver! How cool was that!

"Do you have a passport?" Alex asked.

"Uh, yeah I do. I got it a few years ago for a high school trip to Europe. Only problem is I don't know if I can get the extra time off. I've only been with the bank a couple of months, so I'm not sure how they would react."

"Well, if you can't get the extra time, we could do Friday night through Sunday, yes? I'll get the ticket online and send you the confirmation number. All you have to do is show up at the airport. Have you been to Vancouver before?"

"No, I haven't."

"You'll love it. It's a beautiful city. Okay, let me know what the boss man says and we'll go from there. I'll have some time to spend with you, show you around—my hotel room." He chuckled again. "Just kidding."

Edward said, "I think that will be the part I like best. It's nice being in your house, but I wish you were here with me."

"Me too. Darn..." He paused then said, "Sounds like I have another call coming in. "I'll talk to you later. Take care, Edward, and make yourself at home."

"Thanks. Bye, Alex."

* * * *

Just before six his cell rang again. *Troy.* He was tempted to let the call go to voicemail. *But he might be sick, or something.* "Hi, Troy."

"Where are you?"

"Uh, at a friend's place. What's up?"

"I need a ride tonight."

"You're still going to the party? Troy, that's really not a good idea."

"Hey, I don't need a lecture from you. Kevin's already been up my ass about it. I asked him to take me and he said—before he flounced outta here—he wouldn't be responsible for me getting in with *that crowd* again."

"Then maybe you should listen, Troy. I'm not giving you a ride to some party where you're gonna get wasted and end up in the hospital again."

"Fine, I'll drive myself," Troy rasped, "and if I get in an accident you can congratulate yourself on being a total prick."

"*I'm* a total prick? You need to refine your manners when you're asking for a favor, mister."

"Okay, Southern-fried. Ah forgot you're from the plantation. *Please* take me to the party tonight, Captain Butler, sir."

Despite his annoyance, Edward chuckled at Troy's imitation of Scarlett O'Hara. And he would feel guilty if anything bad did happen to Troy, asshole or not. "Okay, but you have to find a ride back home. I'm not going to stay 'til all hours of the morning."

"What, 'fraid you'll turn into a pumpkin, Cinders? Bring that hunky boyfriend of yours along, or did he dump you already? You were kinda aiming a bit high with that one, don'tcha think?"

"Troy, you are just too mean to be asking for any favors. Find your own way there and back!" He cut the call before Troy could be any more unpleasant. *Man, what a jerk.* His cell rang again immediately, and this time after ascertaining it was Troy, he let it go to voicemail. *Jeez.* His relationships with his roommates had suddenly gone from hardly seeing them to them practically taking over his life. How did that happen?

It only took a moment or two for his conscience to start prickling. What if something did happen to the idiot? Maimed or killed in a road accident, maybe even injuring some innocent bystander. *Shit.* He picked up his cell and punched in Troy's number.

"Okay," he said when Troy's grumpy voice answered, "I'll give you a ride to the party tonight, but promise me you won't get wasted like before."

"I promise, Mother."

"Can you also stop with the snark and show some gratitude, for a change?" Edward asked, with an edge to his voice he hoped would make Troy drop the attitude.

"I will be eternally grateful, O kind sir — and just so you know, I didn't set out to get deliberately wasted the other night. Someone must've slipped me some bad stuff. I mean, who in their right mind wants to end up in the hospital? Can you pick me up at eight?"

"I'll be there," Edward said, trying to ignore the sick feeling in his stomach. *Why, oh why, did I agree to this?*

* * * *

Troy was waiting on the steps outside the apartment building when Edward pulled up. He was wearing a neon green tank top and the tightest pair of jeans Edward had ever seen on any human.

"Nice circumcision," he said dryly when Troy climbed in beside him.

"Eye catching, huh?" Troy leered at him. "Gotta show 'em the goods if you wanna get laid." He checked Edward up and down. "Looks like you're playing it safe. Saving yourself for Mr. TDH?"

"What?" Edward frowned at him as he put the car in gear.

"Tall, Dark and Has-some. I bet he's hung. Is he?"

"Troy, if you're trying to make me feel uncomfortable, you're succeeding. Now change the subject or find another way to get to your party."

Troy slumped back in his seat. "Jesus, go buy yourself a sense of humor, will you? Are you always this uptight?"

"Only around you, it seems. Okay, which way?"

"Take a right to Santa Monica then a left up to Hollywood Boulevard. So I'm guessing he dumped you or he'd be with you tonight."

"Man, you just don't know how to let a thing be, do you?" Edward said through gritted teeth. "Alex is in Vancouver, if you must know, on business, for two weeks."

"Two weeks!" Troy hooted. "Oh, he can get in a lot of trouble in two weeks in Vancouver. That city is full of the best-looking dudes in Canada. Better even than Montreal, and that's saying something."

"You've been there?"

"Oh yeah. Kevin and me went there for Pride a couple of years ago. Oh Mary, we had *the* best time!"

Troy rattled on about how many bars and parties they had gone to and how many incredibly hot men they'd met. As none of it needed an answer or more than the occasional grunt from him, Edward spaced Troy out and started thinking ahead to the weekend when he'd be with Alex in Vancouver. Alex's invitation to join him had given Edward the hope that maybe, just maybe their friendship had a chance of becoming something more meaningful.

But you mustn't put too much emphasis on him asking you up there for the weekend. Just take it easy and don't make more of it than it is – a couple of days and nights together. It did, however, give him the tiniest bit of satisfaction that he'd been asked to join Alex in the city that boasted 'the best-looking dudes in Canada' as Troy had put it.

He was jolted from his reverie when Troy nudged him with his elbow. "Turn left here then keep going up the hill 'til I see the driveway. I think I remember where it is."

Oh, great. The road was narrow with enough sharp curves and bends to rival a corkscrew, and it was dark with no moon at all to give him at least some idea of when the next bend was coming up. He slowed down so Troy could guess at which driveway they should turn.

"I think we passed it," Troy said finally.

"Are you kidding me? D'you have any idea where we're supposed to be going?"

"Well, I got a ride last time, too. I really wasn't paying any attention, I guess."

Edward groaned. "You have their phone number, maybe, so you can call them and ask them for the address?"

"No – shit. Turn back and I'll do a better job of looking this time. I know it wasn't this far up the hill."

Sighing, Edward pulled into the next drive, backed up and did a U-turn onto the narrow road. *If I could have one wish I'd like to be anywhere but here – preferably in Vancouver.*

"Stop," Troy yelled. "I think that's it." He pointed at a dark shape high on the hill to their left.

Edward peered in the direction of Troy's pointing finger. "It doesn't look like anyone's at home."

"Well, they don't exactly advertise there's a party going on. Nosy neighbors. But look, I can see some cars up there. I'm sure this is it."

"Okay." Edward pulled into the driveway and parked behind the last car on the slope. They got out and started walking toward the house. Now Edward could see the glimmer of lights ahead. *They must be using candlelight. Makes sense, I suppose, if they don't want to attract too much attention.* The door was open and he followed Troy inside. Even with the dim lighting Edward could tell the foyer was huge. A few people were moving about and music was playing softly in the background. He heard the clink of glass.

"This way," Troy said, gripping Edward's elbow and steering him into a large room where there were more people and a bar. "Oh, there's Walter. He owns the place. Hey, Walter."

A tall, older man with silver-white hair and a goatee turned and gave Troy a look of no recognition whatsoever. "Hello?"

"Hi, it's Troy, I was here the other night with Pete and Veronica."

Edward could tell Walter had no clue as to who the heck Troy was, but he smiled and gestured toward the bar. "Garth will take care of you." He eyed Edward up and down appraisingly. "Who's your friend?"

"Oh, this is Edward, my roommate. He just migrated from the sticks of North Carolina."

"Really? I'm from North Carolina too, originally." He winked at Edward. "Good place to be from, eh?"

"Sure is." Edward took the man's proffered hand and shivered when his was held just a beat too long. "A drink sounds good." He pulled his hand away and headed for the bar. "I'm having one drink then I'm outta here," he whispered to Troy.

"Oh, *man*," Troy whined.

"Sorry, but this isn't my kind of party." It might just be that he considered himself to be out of his element, but he felt distinctly uncomfortable, a feeling that increased when he noticed a man and a woman having sex and others had gathered around to watch. "Is this some kind of orgy?"

"Naw, they're just high. What'll you have?"

"A beer, thanks."

He found he couldn't take his eyes away from what was going on a few feet away from where they stood at the bar, and he felt ashamed that it fascinated him so much.

"Here." Troy thrust a glass at him. "Drink up. I'll see you around."

"Where are you going?"

"Look up a few friends. I'll be back shortly." He disappeared into a dimly lit hallway.

Edward took a long swallow of his beer. He so didn't want to be here. Maybe he'd find a spot where he could call Alex and tell him what an idiot he'd been to give Troy a ride to this place. Maybe he wouldn't tell him that. He just wanted to hear the sound of his voice.

He slipped his hand into his pocket to get his cell and came up empty. Crap. Had he left it in the car? A naked arm was suddenly snaked round his neck.

"What the hell?"

Laughter followed his startled cry and it was then that he looked down and noticed the arm was covered in tattoos. He was spun round and he sucked in a surprised breath when he encountered Herbie's smirking face, leering at him.

"Hey, country boy, didn't expect to see *you* here. Slumming, are you?"

Edward recovered from his shock at seeing the guy from the Rockin' Bar enough to reply, "Hardly. I don't think Hollywood Hills could be classified as a slum."

"I mean, *this* kind of party. It's all drugs, sex and rock 'n' roll, y'know." Herbie's leer was back.

"Yes, well, I was just about to leave."

"Where's that Martinez guy you were so hot and heavy with at the bar? You and him on the outs already?"

"That isn't any of your business, Herbie." Edward scanned the room to see if Troy was anywhere in sight. *I should let him know I'm leaving.*

"Looking for someone?" Herbie asked, moving closer to Edward.

Edward took a step back. "My roommate. I gave him a ride up here but I'm not staying much longer. I want him to know he'll have to find someone to give him a lift home."

"Is he cute?"

"I guess."

"I've got a car," Herbie said. "Introduce me and I'll offer to take him home."

"I don't see him."

"He's probably in the other party room. I'll show you. In the meantime…" He grabbed Edward's glass. "Let's get you a refill."

"No, that's okay." But Herbie was already at the bar ordering more drinks. He came back carrying two glasses, one of which he handed to Edward.

"Gotcha the good stuff, not the piss they serve the peons. This is Garth's own brew."

"Garth's own brew?"

"Right. Hot, isn't he?"

Edward glanced over at the tall, shirtless, heavily muscled and tattooed man behind the bar, and nodded. "I suppose he is. Friend of yours?"

"On occasion," Herbie replied. "His ink goes all the way down," he added, winking salaciously at Edward. He flexed an arm and a dragon's body writhed over his biceps. "Okay, let's go find your roomie."

Edward took a sip of his drink to prevent it from spilling as they walked down the hall toward where louder music could be heard. Herbie pushed a door open and Edward stood for a moment, transfixed by the sheer number of people crammed into the room. Some were dancing, others making out, and in a far corner, Edward spotted Troy in a huddle with a bunch of other men. He guessed Troy was doing drugs of some kind. He could only hope his roommate wasn't going to overdo it this time around.

"That's Troy, over there, Herbie. The guy wearing the green tank top."

"Oh, he's cute." Herbie's expression had a predatory cast to it. "He's got a ride home. Introduce me."

Navigating across the room through the crush of swaying bodies was difficult, but they finally joined Troy's group and Edward managed to get Troy's attention long enough to tell him Herbie was going to give him a lift home. Troy looked Herbie up and down.

"Cool ink," he said, licking his lips. His eyes were already glazed over.

Edward turned to Herbie. "You sure about this?"

"Totally. Don't worry, I'll take care of him."

"I'm leaving," Edward told Troy. "See you later, and please don't end up in the hospital again."

"Don't worry 'bout me, Southern-fried." Herbie giggled at Troy's nickname for Edward. "My friends here will take good care of me. Run along home and save yourself for your hunky boyfriend who's always out of town."

More giggling ensued. Irritated, and ready to tell Troy just what a jerk he really was, instead Edward turned to go and almost collided with the tall white-haired man Troy had introduced him to earlier. *Walter, that's right.*

"Sorry," he mumbled, holding his beer glass away from Walter's chest.

"Why don't you put that swill down and have a real drink with me before you go?" Walter said smoothly. "We can toast a fond farewell to our home state."

"I really need to get going," Edward replied, moving toward the door.

"Just one." Walter followed him into the hallway. "Where in North Carolina are you from?"

"Ellingsworth."

"Good God." Walter chuckled dryly. "I didn't think that place could produce someone as stunning as you."

They had reached the bar and Edward put his glass down alongside some empty bottles.

"Garth." Walter summoned the bartender over. "Make me and my friend here my favorite cocktail." He squeezed Edward's shoulder. "You'll love this."

Edward was torn between not being rude to the host and getting the hell out of there. His better instincts told him to go, but he sighed inwardly and accepted the small glass Walter handed him.

"Cheers." Walter gave him an urbane smile. "Here's to the many miles that separate us from those we don't miss at all."

Edward grimaced. Not the kind of toast he would have made, but... He sipped the drink. "What is this?"

"Cointreau and bitters. You like it?"

"It's very nice. Different."

"Drink up and we'll have another."

"Oh, no thanks." Edward threw back the rest of the sweet drink then put his glass down on the bar. He caught a glimpse of Troy in the hallway that led to the 'party' room. *Why is he waving at me?* Then Troy disappeared. Edward blinked. *Now I'm seeing things?* "Thank you, Walter, but I really must go. It was a pleasure meeting you."

"And you, Edward. I think we'll meet again very soon."

"Goodnight." He turned and walked across the room toward the entryway. His legs began to feel like lead weights and his head spun. He leaned against a wall, trying to stop the dizziness that threatened to overcome him. He couldn't put one foot in front of the other. He sank to his knees. *What's happening?* He fell forward onto the hard, wooden floor. *Somebody help...me...*

He was dimly aware of someone lifting him to his feet and dragging him forward. Voices, seeming to come from far away, made a vague impression on his mind. One voice, louder than the others, sounded close to his ear. *Troy?* Someone was pulling at him, he wanted to scream at them to let him go. A long, violent shudder racked his body. He went completely limp as he gave himself up to the darkness.

C h a p t e r   S e v e n

Three days later

Alex closed his phone and sighed. Okay, that made three times today he'd called Edward with no response. He'd left messages yesterday and the day before, and—nothing. He was worried, frustrated too because he didn't have either of Edward's roommates' phone numbers. He didn't even know their last names so couldn't do a directory search. Could it be that Edward was deliberately ignoring his calls? It was a possibility, of course, yet he'd have sworn that Edward was as interested in prolonging their friendship as he was.

So what was going on? He glanced at his watch. Ten o'clock—there was a good chance Blanca might be at his house. *Worth a try.* He speed-dialed his cleaning lady's number. Even if she wasn't there right then, she might have been in the past couple of days. He never could remember her schedule anyway.

"*Si?*" Blanca answered on the third ring.

"Oh, hi, Blanca, it's Alex."

"Señor Alex. *Como esta?*

"*Muy bien, gracias,* Blanca. Are you over at my place right now?"

"*Si,* you want me to do something *especial?*"

"No, I have a friend staying there… Edward. Have you seen him?"

"No, but someone has been here," she replied in her careful English. "There is a cell phone on the countertop. He must have left it behind."

That explains why he hasn't returned my calls, but why hasn't he been back for it? "Has the bed been slept in?"

"Not unless he left it *exactamente* like I make it. No, I would say it has not been slept in."

Damn, now I'm worried. "Okay, thanks, Blanca."

"What should I do about the phone?"

"Just leave it there. He has a key, so in case he comes looking for it…"

"*Si,* I'll leave it."

After they'd hung up Alex considered calling the local hospital in West Hollywood or the police precinct, but just then he was distracted by a knocking and Lena's voice calling, "Alex, are you there?"

Groaning, he hurried to the door and opened it. Lena was, as she had been off and on since he'd arrived, in tears. She brushed by him and threw herself onto the nearby couch.

"I can't do this movie, Alex, I just can't," she sobbed, clutching her cream-colored silk robe about her. "That son of a bitch Harrison is making my life a misery."

No, you're making all our lives a misery. His expression did not reflect his weary thought. Being around Lena for the past seventy-two hours had been a nightmare. Working with her must be total hell. He'd seen the looks of anguish and frustration on her co-actors' faces. As for Will Harrison, the director — he'd appeared to be either suicidal or homicidal—Alex wasn't sure which—the last time he'd seen him storming off the set.

"He's making me do the same scene over and over until I'm ready to scream."

"He's a perfectionist." Alex sat beside her on the couch. "Will just wants to make sure you give your very best."

"I've given him all I can, Alex. I called Jeff and told him I don't want to do this anymore."

"But the studio will sue, Lena." Alex sighed but tried to hide his exasperation. "Jeff won't agree to you quitting the film. It'll give you a bad reputation for being difficult to work with. Just take it easy, get to bed early tonight. No drinking, no pills, no parties. When shooting's done for the day, we'll go for a nice dinner and—"

"No, Alex, no!" Lena stood and paced around the room, running her hands through her long auburn hair. "I want you to call the airline and reserve us three seats back to Los Angeles. If Will Harrison wants me so badly for his film, then he can come shoot the damn thing there."

"But economically—"

"I don't give a damn about the fact it's cheaper to make movies in Canada. I want to go home. If Hank were still alive he'd never put me through something like this. He'd— Oh, God, I miss him so. And I know you do too. Why do you never want to talk about him? Are you still in love with him, Alex?" She flung herself down on the couch again and stared at him weepily through her smudged mascara. "You still blame me for his death, don't you?"

"No, of course I don't, Lena." God, but he so didn't need this right now. "I don't think it's good for you to constantly talk about him, that's all. You have to let him go, move on with your life. You need this movie to put you back on track."

"But the media won't let me forget him, Alex. That horrible report about the incident in your office had them showing news clips from the night he died."

"You shouldn't have watched any of that crap." He'd asked Sophia to make sure none of the TV sets in her dressing room or hotel room were tuned in to the tabloid newscasts, but she'd seen it the night before he'd arrived, and hadn't stopped talking about it ever since.

"Just call the airline, will you please?" She slumped back into the couch pillows and closed her eyes. "And tell Sophia we're leaving."

Sighing, Alex picked up his cell and punched in Scott's number. He and Jeff, Lena's agent, were just going to love this, and no doubt Jeff would want to blame him for not doing a better job of controlling Lena's tantrums. Maybe it was time to look for a new job.

* * * *

Edward opened his eyes and stared at the unfamiliar ceiling with its overly bright fluorescent light. *Where the hell am I?* He moved his head to the right a little and took in the sterile surroundings. *Shit, a hospital room. But why?* He ached all over and when he glanced down he could see his arms were bandaged. *Jeez, was I in a car accident or something?* He had no memory of that. In fact the last thing he did remember was being at that awful party with Troy. And he'd been going to leave to do *something...*

That's right, look for my phone so I could call Alex. Alex... Does he know I'm in this hospital? I've got a date with him in Vancouver. I remember that all right.

He glanced toward the door as it opened and a nurse peeked in. She smiled on seeing he was awake. "Good morning, Edward, how are you feeling today?" she asked just a little too brightly.

"Okay, I guess. I'm just not sure what happened, why I'm here."

"You've been unconscious for three days." She walked over to the bed and began checking the levels on the IVs attached to him. "I'll let the doctor know you're awake so he can give you a proper diagnosis."

"Was I in a car accident?"

"We're not sure. You were found on the side of the road in Hollywood Hills — but the doctor will give you the details. He'll be here in a few minutes. Do you feel like having something to eat?"

"Maybe just some water. My mouth feels like it's full of sand."

She nodded and filled a sippy-cup with water. "Here you go." She held the straw to his lips. "Can you manage? Be careful when you move your arm. You have quite a lot of cuts and bruises."

He winced as he moved to hold the cup. What the hell had happened? He couldn't remember anything that might have led to having an accident — car or otherwise.

"I'll hold it for you if it hurts to move," the nurse said. "I'm Joan by the way."

"Thanks, Joan. I think I can manage."

"Good. I'll just go and get the doctor so he can fill you in on the details I'm sure you can't wait to know." She gave him another bright smile then left.

Edward was quietly stunned by this development. In the back of his mind he sensed that whatever had happened to him was not of his own volition. He'd been with Troy, had driven him to the party — so where was his car? If he'd been in a wreck, surely he would remember actually driving his car away from the party, with or without Troy. He knew he hadn't been entirely comfortable with what was going on. Troy had got him a beer, then disappeared, and...? There was nothing after that. He'd wanted to call Alex.

He looked up as a tall, fairly young man, wearing dark horn-rimmed glasses, entered the room.

"Good morning, Edward, I'm Doctor Wingate. I'd offer to shake your hand but I think that might still be a little painful for you."

"What happened, Doctor?" Edward asked, trying to put his cup of water to one side. Wingate stepped forward and took it from his hand, placing it on the tray next to his bed.

"You've been in some kind of accident. At least we think it was an accident. You were found lying in the road by a lady driving her car on Laurel Drive. She called nine-one-one and waited with you until the paramedics arrived. You were in pretty bad shape when you were admitted here. Fortunately most of your injuries are superficial — cuts and bruises, a whack on the head, that kind of thing. You did some damage to your knees, but nothing's broken. You'll heal in a week or two." He paused and his expression grew solemn.

"But there's something else, isn't there," Edward said, with a sinking feeling in his stomach.

"I'm afraid so. We did a blood analysis and it showed positive for Rohypnol."

"What's that?"

"Its more common term is 'roofie', or 'date rape drug'."

Edward stared up at Wingate, the queasy feeling in his stomach now churning to the point where he thought he might throw up.

"I was raped?" He could barely get the words out. "Oh, my God."

Wingate put a calming hand on Edward's shoulder. "No, you were not raped, Edward. In cases like this it's usual to medically examine the victim, and I can assure you, you were not violated in that manner."

Edward didn't know which emotion of the many that swamped his psyche at that moment was the most powerful. Relief at the knowledge he hadn't been sexually molested, that there was no danger of him having contracted HIV, or the deep, burning anger that started to build inside him at the realization that someone had done this to him – had drugged him in order to – do what? And why was he so banged up? Why had he been found lying on the side of the road? Who the hell had done this?

Well, there was one person who just might have some idea – *Troy*.

He became aware that Wingate was still talking. He'd been so chewed up by his emotional reactions he'd tuned the doctor out. "I'm sorry, what did you say?"

"I asked if there was someone we could contact to apprise of your situation. You have a North Carolina driver's license. I understand the police tried calling the phone number they linked to your home address, but so far no one has responded."

What a surprise. I could be at death's door and my family still doesn't give a shit about me.

He blinked away the tears welling in his eyes. "No, there's no one." He certainly wasn't going to have them contact his roommates. He'd deal with them when he got released from the hospital. "Wait, I have a friend, but he's in Vancouver right now. Maybe you could let him know?"

"Sure. Do you have his phone number?"

"Uh, it's on my cell."

"I'm afraid there was no cell phone among your personal items. No cell and no car keys."

Damn. He struggled to recall what he'd assigned to speed dial once he and Alex had exchanged numbers. "I think it's five-five-five thirty eight hundred. His name is Alex Martinez. Oh, and maybe someone could call the bank where I work. They've probably fired me by now for not showing up or calling."

Wingate took the name of the bank and said he'd have one of the nurses call both numbers as soon as possible.

"When will I be released?" Edward asked.

"Another day or so. It takes time for the drug to completely leave your system, especially the large dose you were given, mixed with alcohol. You can suffer from disorientation and a tendency to fall asleep. Now that you're awake the police will want a statement from you."

"The police?"

"Yes, Edward. You are the victim of a crime, so they'll want the details, or as much as you can remember. In the meantime, we'll keep you on the pain meds and get you some real food to build up your strength." He made some notations on the iPad he carried. "I'll look in on you later today."

After the doctor had left, Edward closed his eyes and let the full weight of his situation fill his mind.

He'd been unconscious for three days. If they were including Saturday in that number it meant he'd only missed one day of work so far. Maybe once someone from the hospital called, his boss wouldn't fire him out of hand. If they got a hold of Alex, he might call him here. He would really love to hear Alex's deep, soothing voice, but more than anything, he wished Alex were here with him now. It was silly, he knew, to put so much faith in Alex's ability to make things better, but right now, what he felt was, vulnerable… *alone.*

The police had called his parents and they hadn't bothered to find out if he was okay.

How in hell did I ever become a product of such a cold, unfeeling bunch? If my son were hospitalized, I'd be at his side day and night.

Once again, tears formed behind his eyelids, and he blinked them away impatiently. There was no point in grieving over the lost love of his family. There never would be a happy reconciliation. Not now. Not ever.

* * * *

Alex sighed with relief after he had deposited Lena back in her Beverly Hills home. The flight from Vancouver had felt like the longest trip in the world. Lena was losing it, without a doubt, but with Jeff waiting for her at her home, Alex had decided it was better if he wasn't around for their 'talk'. He was expected back at the office for a meeting with Scott, but first, he wanted to check up on Edward.

Probably the best place to start is at his apartment.

He took a cab from Lena's to his house so he could pick up his car. He went inside just in case Edward was there, even though there was no sign of his car in the driveway. His cell phone was still on the counter so Alex pocketed it before he left. There was no doubt in his mind now that something bad had happened. Maybe he'd gotten the flu, or food poisoning?

Just as he was about to get in his car, his cell phone chimed. "Alex Martinez." He answered the call without checking the ID.

"Oh, Mr. Martinez, my name is Joan. I'm a nurse at Saint Patrick's Hospital. We have a patient here, an Edward Conway, who says you're a friend. He knows you're in Vancouver but just wanted you to know where he is."

Hospital? "Yes, yes, I know him. Is he all right?"

"He's improving. He was unconscious for a time, but he's awake now. Perhaps you can come see him when you're back in town."

"I'll be right there," Alex said and hung up. Despite his worry over Edward's condition, he smiled wryly as he thought of Joan the nurse's surprise when he said he'd be right there. Vancouver to LA in twenty minutes or so. He'd tell her he doubled as The Flash in his spare time, if she asked.

* * * *

When he arrived at the nurses' station at Saint Patrick's and asked to see Edward he was told he'd have to wait as there was a detective in the room getting a statement from the patient.

"Detective?" Alex exclaimed. "What happened to him?"

Before the nurse could reply, a tall bespectacled man who had been scribbling something on a pad turned to him and said, "I'm Doctor Wingate. You're a friend of Edward's?"

"Yes, Alex Martinez."

The doctor's expression showed his surprise. "Edward told us you were in Vancouver."

"Yes, my trip got cut short. What happened to him?"

"He was drugged and left lying on the roadside. He has no memory of what took place, but happily his injuries aren't too severe."

"Drugged. My God." Alex immediately recalled Troy's invitation to a party he'd described as having 'all the drugs and sex you need'. Had Edward gone to the party? He couldn't imagine him being a part of something so seedy, and he hadn't mentioned going when he'd dropped Alex off at the airport. But what did he really know about Edward? They'd only been seeing each other for just over a week, and he'd been gone for most of the time.

"Can I see him?" he asked.

"Once the police are out of there, yes." Doctor Wingate gave Alex an appraising look. "Just so you know, they tried to contact his family in North Carolina. There has been no response from them."

Alex grimaced. "He parted from them on bad terms."

"Came out to them, I expect?" Wingate's tone was gentle.

Alex nodded. "They gave him a rough time from what he told me."

"Not unusual. He's going to need a lot of TLC to help him overcome the trauma of his experience. Are you and he lovers?"

"We've only been seeing each other a short time, and my job took me away for a good amount of that time, but I'd say we're close, yes."

"Good, he'll need that."

They both watched as a wide-shouldered, sandy-haired man approached the station.

"Did he manage to remember anything else, Detective?" Wingate asked.

"Not enough to help find out who did this to him. He did give me the approximate location of the house where he said the party was held. Didn't know the actual address as his roommate was directing and got lost a couple of times. We'll check the neighborhood and see if anyone recalls hearing a party going on nearby."

"Have you questioned his roommate?" Alex asked.

The detective flicked hazel eyes his way and gave Alex the once-over. "And you are?"

"Alex Martinez. I'm a friend of Edward's."

"Detective McLennan." He didn't offer a handshake. "Were you at this party?"

"No, I was in Vancouver, and I'd hazard a guess Edward was only there because Troy asked him for a ride to the party."

"Well…" McLennan tapped his iPad and glanced at the screen. "He was able to give me the address of his apartment and his roommates' names. Troy is the one you mentioned, so we'll have a talk with him first." He turned to the doctor. "Are you releasing him any time soon?"

"Tomorrow maybe, if he keeps showing improvement. There's a tendency for some people to feel the effects of the drug for a few days. Being unable to stay awake can be a lingering result."

"These injuries he's sustained—they don't really line up with being hit by a car." McLennan gave Wingate a questioning look. "Would you agree?"

The doctor nodded. "Yes, it's more like he fell then rolled over and over. His knees might have taken the brunt of the fall."

"Like he fell, jumped, or was pushed out of a car?"

"That's a possibility."

"I'm going with the fact that the last thing he remembers is being in the house, yet he's found on the roadside. A car seems the obvious choice to me. Is it possible for him to have realized what was happening and tried to get away even in his drugged state?"

"It's possible. There can be moments of lucidity shortly after the drug is ingested."

"Okay, thanks, Doc. I know where to find him if we need any more info from him." He gave them both a brief nod then headed for the elevator.

"He seems efficient enough," Alex remarked. "Can I go see Edward now?"

"Yes, go ahead." Wingate smiled. "I think you'll be a better tonic for him than anything we can give him. Room six eighteen."

"Thanks, Doctor."

Alex hurried down the corridor, scanning the room numbers as he went. He knocked softly on Edward's door and peeked in. "Are you open for visitors?" he whispered.

"Alex! But how — ?" The smile on Edward's face that expressed just how much he was pleased to see him made Alex's heart quiver.

"The trip was cut short due to the star's reluctance to cooperate." He grinned at Edward then leaned down to kiss his lips gently. His expression clouded when he noticed the bandages on Edward's arms. "What happened, Edward?"

Edward sighed. "I wish I knew."

Alex pulled the chair by the bed closer, and held Edward's hand. "The cop said you went to that party Troy was raving about."

"Yeah, he coerced me into driving him up there. I should have been mean like Kevin, but I caved when he said he'd drive there himself and I would have to live with the guilt if he got into an accident. It was awful, Alex, what I remember of it. I had a beer, then I was going to call you, but I couldn't find my cell."

"You left it at my place, on the counter," Alex told him. He dug it out of his pocket. "It most likely needs charging. You'll hear a ton of messages from me. I was worried about you." He squeezed Edward's hand. "Damned Troy. He's gonna hear it from me when I see him."

"What's the point? He'll never change. Alex..." Edward curled his fingers round Alex's. "Someone put a roofie in my drink. It might have been Troy, although maybe that's going a bit too far, even for him. He got me a beer. It was so dark in the house, I really couldn't make out what was going on at first, then I saw a couple having sex with a bunch of people standing around watching and getting off on it. The visual was erotic, but there was something off about it. I'm not a prude, but... Hey, I made out with you on the dance floor remember?"

"I remember." Alex raised Edward's hand to his lips and kissed the palm. "When you're feeling a hundred percent again, we have a dance date."

Edward smiled. "Soon as I get out of here." His face clouded as he remembered. "Then Herbie—you remember the tattooed guy from the bar? He got me another beer, but I didn't drink much of it. It tasted funny. He said it was Garth's special brew, whatever that meant."

"Who's Garth?"

"The bartender. Herbie wanted to meet Troy so we went into another room. It was packed with people dancing. Anyway I left Herbie with Troy, then this other guy, who owned the place, said he was from North Carolina and we should have a drink together. I told him I was leaving but he persisted and finally I just gave in so I could get away. I started to leave, and I'm afraid that's about all I remember. I just wish I could remember what happened that left me lying on the side of the road."

"The cop asked Doctor Wingate if it was possible you fell or jumped out of a car. D'you have any recollection of that?"

"Not really. I keep getting flashes of stuff, like when that detective was asking me questions, I thought I had an answer that could maybe help, but then it sort of vanished." He yawned. "Sorry, I keep wanting to fall asleep, but I don't want to while you're here."

Alex smiled gently. "That's okay, the doc said you'll be woozy for a while until the drug leaves your system. You sleep and I'll come back later. I have a meeting with Scott, but I'll tell you all about that when you're more up to listening." He kissed Edward's forehead. "Okay, get some shuteye."

"'Kay. I'm glad you're back, Alex."

"So am I."

* * * *

For the next few hours, Edward dozed off and on, sometimes slipping into a heavy sleep, only to awake with a start, still surprised by his surroundings. Apart from the nurses' frequent checking and Doctor Wingate's follow-up visit, he was left pretty much on his own, which gave him time to think. His last lucid memory at the party was accepting the drink from Walter, but he was having snatches of other memories. Sometimes they involved Troy, but unfortunately they were always too fleeting to hang onto, or make anything of.

He knew he had searched for his cell phone, then decided he must have left it in the car—but did he ever reach his car in order to look? He couldn't remember the walk to where his car was parked, yet he had some kind of residual memory of being in the vehicle, but on the passenger side. Why the hell would he have been sitting there—unless he'd reached over to search for his cell and had fallen onto the seat?

The detective had told him that so far there was no report of his car being found, either abandoned or in an accident. Was it still on the driveway of the party house, or had Troy used it to get home? The doc had said his car keys were missing along with his cell. Well, at least Alex had brought his cell phone back to him. Could Troy have taken his car keys while he lay there unconscious? If so, why hadn't he driven him back to the apartment? Was Troy that much of a jerk that he'd just leave him behind? Wait, Herbie had said he'd drive Troy home. Anything could have happened between those two. They may have gone to Herbie's place. Did Troy even know, or care, what had happened?

Maybe if Detective McLennan gets some answers he'll be able to throw some light on what went down that night.

* * * *

By the time Alex got to work, Lena's agent, Jeff Harding, was already seated in Scott's office and looking decidedly grim. Scott waved Alex over to a seat while Jeff glared at him. Alex sighed. He was getting used to Jeff's dirty looks, but he was not going to take the blame for Lena's decision to walk out of the movie production in Vancouver.

"Morning," he said as he sat in front of Scott's desk.

"Morning, Alex," Scott replied, while Jeff grunted something indistinguishable. "So, Alex, not a good time in Vancouver, huh?"

"Lena is in a bad frame of mind. She's feeling very vulnerable right now, and for some reason doesn't want to be away from LA. She's still grieving in a way, and —"

Jeff snorted angrily. "Grieving, my ass. She's a fucking manic depressive, and the drugs she takes only makes it worse. You were supposed to be up there making sure she was fit for work every day, and you let her persuade you to bring her back home. You let her walk out of a mega-million dollar movie production!"

"And just exactly how was I going to stop her, Jeff?" Alex controlled his voice, although he really wanted to give Jeff a piece of his mind. In Alex's opinion, Jeff had no conception as to what really bothered Lena, nor did he have the compassion to actually care. "Lena was in no mood to listen to reason from me or anyone else. You were with her this morning. How did she seem to you? Calm and reasonable, ready to go back to work?"

Jeff turned his glare on Scott. "You gonna let him talk to me like that?"

"Calm down, Jeff," Scott said mildly. "We all know dealing with Lena can tax the patience of the strongest man. Blaming Alex for Lena's decisions isn't going to solve the problem."

"Then what is?" Jeff demanded.

"Maybe you can get Will Harrison to shoot the scenes he doesn't need Lena in," Alex said quietly, "then finish the movie here in LA. Will knows what he's got in Lena. She's still an enormous box office draw. He's not going to want to throw away what he's already created."

"Did you see any of the rushes, Alex?" Scott asked.

Alex nodded. "Yeah, and they're very good. Honestly?" He directed his gaze at Jeff. "I can't see Will firing her, even though he was threatening to do just that when we left."

Jeff groaned. "I've been fielding his calls all morning."

"Speak to him," Alex said. "You're Lena's agent. You know how to sell talent, and you won't have to work too hard on this. I bet he's already making the decision to wrap what he has and move the production to LA."

"You think?" Jeff didn't quite sneer the words but he didn't look too happy either.

"Worth a try," Scott said, shrugging slightly. "Anyway, Alex, thanks for getting Lena back home safely. And think of it this way, Jeff, she's garnered some free publicity for the movie."

"Yeah, yeah, yeah."

Alex tuned out the rest of the conversation. His thoughts had already turned back to Edward in the hospital and wanting to know who could have done this criminal thing to him. *Well, it doesn't look like I'm going to lose my job, so...* "If you don't mind, gentlemen." He got to his feet. "I have some work I need to take care of. I'll check in with Lena later in the day. Okay?"

Jeff grunted. He was good at that, but Scott smiled and said, "Talk at you later, Alex."

"Later, Scott." He got up and left the room, then headed for his own office down the hall. He'd no sooner got there when his cell phone chimed. He glanced at the text on the screen, and heaved a sigh. *Lena…*

Need you to come back. I feel like ending it all. Please come over. Please, Alex.

He texted back. *On my way.*

He stopped in at Scott's office where Jeff was just about to leave.

"I have to go over to Lena's, she threatening again."

"Shit." Jeff scowled at him. "I'll go. You'll just mollycoddle her. She needs to learn the facts of life—one being that her career will go up in fucking smoke if she doesn't pull herself together."

"Don't be rough with her," Alex said. "She's—"

"I know what she is," Jeff snapped at him. "And telling her everything will be okay won't help. She needs to quit with the drama and knuckle under like everyone else—if she wants to keep her career going." He gave Alex an unpleasant look. "Maybe you should stay away from her. You're too soft—"

"Make up your mind, Jeff." Alex met the agent's aggressive stance without backing down. "One minute you're demanding I go to Vancouver to be with her, and now you want me to stay away. Are you sure *you* know what's best for Lena?"

"Don't talk to me like that." He glared over at Scott. "Are you allowing this?"

"Alex is right," Scott said mildly. "Lena relies on him as a friend. She doesn't need to be intimidated right now."

"I'm not intimidating her," Jeff barked, his face flushing with anger. "I'm trying to save her career!"

"How about trying to save Lena?" Alex asked.

"Okay, I've had enough of this shit from you." Jeff stalked out of the office. He paused at the doorway and sneered at them. "As of now, the Scott Malone Agency no longer represents Lena Miles. You got that? You're fired — and *you*..." He pointed a finger at Alex's chest. "You will keep your faggoty nose out of her, and my, business!"

Alex suppressed the angry retort that had sprung to his lips. He stared at the anxious faces of the other employees and knew a nasty back and forth with Jeff Harding wasn't going to accomplish a thing. He watched him slam through the glass doors and march toward the elevators.

"Good riddance," Scott muttered.

"Lena won't let him fire you," Alex told him. He dropped into the seat Jeff had just vacated. "She's not going to be happy with Jeff going over to her house instead of me. I'll let her know he's on his way." He punched in a quick text telling her what had happened and that he'd call her later. "I would just love to know who the hell leaked the story of her getting pepper-sprayed in this office. I thought we had a group of pretty loyal people here."

He raised an eyebrow when he caught Scott squirming uncomfortably in his chair. "C'mon, Scott, you know something about this, don't you. Who was it?"

"Fuck. This can't go any further than this office. It was me."

"*What?*" Alex stared incredulously at his boss.

"Well, not exactly me." He sighed and looked away guiltily. "I told Gloria and she told that group she hangs out with—you know, they all like to think they're the *Housewives of Beverly Hills*. All they do is sit around and dish all day…"

"Scott, you're being extremely sexist," Alex said, trying not to laugh.

"Maybe. Anyway, one of them blabbed to a reporter friend, and that was that. I told Glory she'd almost lost me a client—I didn't tell her I was ready to disassociate our agency from Lena before the pepper-spraying incident. Had to make her feel really guilty, y'know."

"Well, I'm just glad it wasn't one of ours." Alex shook his head at Scott. "Can I say I'm really surprised at you?"

"Razz me all you like," Scott said, grimacing. "I fucked up, but my wife never gets any more scoops about what goes on here."

Alex laughed and stood up. "Well, I better get some work done."

"Hey, Alex…" Scott gave him a wry smile. "Just so you know, I appreciate all you do here. And don't worry about Jeff. His opinion means nothing to me. You're my friend as well as my employee."

"Thanks, boss." He grinned at Scott. "I love you too."

Chapter Eight

Detective Mark McLennan checked the apartment number with the one he'd noted on his iPad then knocked sharply on the door. A few seconds later the door was flung open and a slim, auburn-haired man stared at him, his eyes widening with interest as he took in McLennan's good looks.

"Mr. Kendall?"

The man shook his head vigorously. "No, he's not here right now. Haven't seen him in about two or three days."

"Since Saturday night, maybe?"

"Yeah, that's right."

"Your name, sir?"

"Uh, Kevin Marshall."

"And your other roommate is Edward Conway?"

"That's right. What's going on? You wanna come in?"

McLennan nodded and stepped inside. Kevin closed the door behind him then gestured at the couch, but McLennan shook his head. "I prefer to stand. You can sit down if you like."

Kevin plunked himself down on the couch and looked up at McLennan expectantly. "So what's happened to them?"

"Mr. Conway is in the hospital. He was drugged and left on the side of the road up in Hollywood Hills."

"Jesus." Kevin stared at McLennan with a shocked expression. "He must have gone with Troy to that party I wouldn't take him to."

"Were you not concerned that both your roommates were missing?"

Kevin shrugged. "Well, Ed's been seeing some new boyfriend so I figured they were spending time together, and Troy? Well, frankly he's done this before. Not for as long, a day or two, maybe, but he runs around with people I don't care for."

"This party, do you know the address of the house it was being held in?"

"No, and I'm really surprised Ed would go with Troy."

"Mr. Conway says Mr. Kendall more or less coerced him into giving him a ride to the party. As far as he recalls he was about to leave when he passed out. He has no memory of what happened after that. The doctor says he was given a dose of Rohypnol, the date rape drug." He paused as Kevin gasped. "He was not sexually molested but it's obvious he'd either been in a fall or suffered some injuries in some other manner. Without his remembering what happened, we can't be sure how he came by the injuries."

"And Troy?"

"Mr. Kendall is still missing. Are there friends he might be with—or family?"

"He works for Truegate Travel, but they haven't called asking where he is. His parents live in Texas, and he's not in touch with them too often. He has a brother somewhere in California, but I'm not sure exactly where. And other friends? I don't really know who he sees. We go to the movies together sometimes, but apart from me, just those guys who'd have been at the party. I don't know if you could really call them friends."

"Are you and Mr. Kendall partners?"

"No, we went to school together back in Odessa, that's all."

"Do you have a photograph of Mr. Kendall I could have?"

"Uh, yeah sure." Kevin got up and walked over to a bookshelf, returning with a group photo of four smiling young men. "That's Troy on my left. Cute, isn't he?"

McLennan ignored the sly grin on Kevin's face. "Do you know a person called…" He glanced at his iPad. "Herbie? Mr. Conway described him as short and covered in tattoos."

Kevin laughed. "I don't *know* him. I've seen him at the Rockin' Bar. He's kinda hard to miss, but I'm surprised Ed would be hanging out with him. Herbie's not his type at all."

"You know his last name?"

"Not a clue."

McLennan pocketed his iPad along with the photograph. "Well, thank you, Mr. Marshall. If you hear from Mr. Kendall, let him know we need to talk to him right away. He might be able to throw some light on what happened on Saturday night."

"Is Ed going to be all right?"

McLennan nodded. "Physically yes, but there might be some trauma from the experience."

"Shit. I should probably go visit him. He's in St. Patrick's?"

"Yes. Room six eighteen."

"Okay. Uh, maybe I'll text him instead."

McLennan gave him a long look before turning toward the door. "You might want to consider an actual visit. Have a nice day, Mr. Marshall."

* * * *

Alex paused in the hospital lobby as his cell rang. He sighed when he saw Lena's name on the ID screen. "Hi, Lena."

"You were supposed to be coming over here, and I got Jeff instead." He could hear the annoyance in her voice.

"I texted you to let you know. He didn't want me interfering, said I was too soft with you."

"He wants me to fire Scott."

"And what do you want, Lena?" Alex walked over to a bench near the elevator and sat down.

"Oh, I don't care who does my publicity, you know that, but you work for Scott so I told Jeff he couldn't fire him. He left in a temper. Can you come see me now?"

"I'm on my way to see a friend in the hospital."

"Oh, what's wrong?"

"He was in an accident, but he'll be okay, according to the doctor. I just want to go visit with him, see if he needs anything."

"Are you dating him?" There was a sudden sharp edge to Lena's tone.

"We've been out a couple of times, yes, but as you know I've been out of town for several days so I wouldn't actually call it dating." He tried for a lighter mood. "I'm not sure what constitutes dating these days. I've been out of the loop for a long time."

"You once told me no one could ever replace Hank in your life."

"And no one can, Lena. I'm not looking for a replacement for Hank."

"Alex, please come over. I need you here. I have all these decisions to make, and I need your help."

"What decisions?"

"Oh, whether to continue with the movie, that kind of thing."

"Of course you must finish the movie. Surely Jeff is taking care of that with the studio?"

"I suppose he is, but there's something I need to discuss with you."

"Tell me what it is."

"When you're here. You are coming over, aren't you?"

"Later, Lena." He glanced at his watch. "I'm going to visit my friend first."

"Oh, now he's more important to you than I am? We've been friends for years, Alex, and suddenly some guy you picked up in a bar is your priority?"

Alex couldn't deny the 'picked up in a bar' part of what she'd just said, but having Edward described as 'some guy' didn't sit at all well with him. In his gut, he already knew Edward was more than just some bar pickup. He'd had those over the past year or so, and they'd been just that, and even though he and Edward hadn't had a chance to know each other very well yet, seeing him lying in that hospital bed had stirred something inside him. Something he hadn't felt in a long, long time. Ever since…

"Alex, are you still there?" Lena's anxious voice shook him from his thoughts.

"Yes, still here, but I have to go, Lena."

"No, no wait, Alex, please. What I have to tell you is that Jeff wants me to marry again. He says the publicity is just what I need — it'll boost the movie's ratings."

"Wow, Lena, I didn't know you'd been seeing someone. Who is it?"

He could sense her impatience even without seeing her. "There isn't anyone — of course there isn't anyone, except in Jeff's mind," she snapped. "If I'd been seeing someone, you'd be the first to know. He wants me to start dating Ryan Hart, be seen with him at parties and galas, that kind of thing. This will be an arranged marriage."

Just like with Hank. Except that Lena had really loved Hank. *Ryan Hart.* As far as he knew Hart was straight, so at least this wouldn't be an arrangement to save his reputation.

"Well, the dating part may not be so bad, Lena. He's a nice-looking guy and he's big in the industry right now. Maybe you'll enjoy going out with him."

The sigh that filled his ear was long and overly dramatic. "All right, Alex, go see your friend. I can tell I'm not high on the list of people you care about."

"Lena, that's ridiculous, and you know darn well it's not true. I'll call you later." He hung up before their conversation deteriorated further.

Lena, Lena. I really wish you'd meet someone who would free you from the past.

* * * *

Edward looked up and his heart quickened when the gentle knock on the door was followed by Alex stepping into the room, his face wreathed in smiles. "Hi."

"Hi yourself." Alex leaned down to brush his lips over Edward's. "How are you feeling?"

"Better now you're here." He reached up to cup the back of Alex's head and hold him in place for a longer kiss.

Alex sat on the side of the bed and slipped an arm under Edward's shoulders to support him. "How tight can I hug you?" he whispered.

"Tight as you like." He opened to Alex's exploring tongue and shivered with pleasure as the warm, moist flesh caressed the inside of his mouth. "Mmm…" He moaned and Alex pulled back a little to meet his longing gaze with a smile.

"Edward, when they release you, I think you should come stay with me. You'll need some aftercare for a few days, and I don't think your roomies can be relied on to do that."

"Are you sure?" Edward was inwardly delighted that Alex cared enough to go out of his way like this. He really hadn't been relishing the idea of going back to the apartment, but at the same time, he didn't want to put a strain on their very new friendship. "I don't want to be a burden, Alex."

"You won't be, so just say yes and I'll get the guest room set up for you."

"The guest room." Edward couldn't quite keep the disappointment out of his voice.

"Just 'til you're feeling better," Alex said, chuckling. "As much as I want to ravish you again, it might be a good idea to wait until those cuts and bruises heal."

Edward smiled. "Ravish me. I like the sound of that."

They both looked up as Doctor Wingate entered the room. Alex stood and after shaking hands with the doctor, moved to the other side of the bed. Edward couldn't help noticing that the doctor's gaze was fixed firmly on Alex's nicely rounded butt before making eye contact with Edward.

"You certainly appear a lot better than you did this morning," he said after a quick inspection of the bruising around Edward's neck and chest. "I think maybe just one more day of observation and we can send you home. We got in touch with your employer, and he said for you to bring a note from us when you're ready to go back to work. So no worries there, eh?"

"Thanks, Doctor."

"You will need some help getting around for a couple of days. Is there someone at home who can do that?"

"He's staying with me until he's fit," Alex said, "so yes, he'll have someone to look after him. I have a housekeeper who can come in if I'm at work, but I intend taking some time off, so it shouldn't be a problem."

"Good." Wingate checked the readout he carried. "Your latest blood work shows no trace of the Rohypnol in your system, so you should feel much stronger and more alert by tomorrow. Just take it easy, keep those knees iced for a few days and you'll be fine." He smiled at them both. "I think you'll be in very good hands when we release you."

Alex sat back down on the side of Edward's bed after Wingate had left. "Methinks the doctor is gay."

"Yeah, and methinks he'd really like to be in your very good hands," Edward said, trying to pull Alex down for a kiss.

"Jealous?" Alex teased him by giving his nose a peck instead.

"I could be. I don't want to have to share you with anyone this soon."

"No fear of that." Alex covered Edward's mouth with his, pushing gently inside with the tip of his tongue, but their moment of pleasure was disrupted by another knock at the door. This time it was Kevin.

"Oh, hi, Kevin." Edward was surprised at the visit, but tried to sound pleased.

"Hey, how are you? Hope I didn't interrupt anything." Kevin's smirk belied his words as his gaze fell on Alex. "Hi, I'm Kevin, you must be Alex."

Alex stood and politely shook the proffered hand. "Any word of Troy?" he asked.

Kevin stopped leering long enough to shake his head and assume a sad expression. "No. A cop came by with a bunch of questions, and told me—jeez, Edward, I just couldn't believe it when he said you'd been drugged and dumped out on the street. You don't remember anything at all?"

"Not so far." Edward watched with some amusement as Kevin stepped closer to Alex who promptly sat back down on the bed and pointed to a chair in the corner.

"You can bring that over here if you like," Alex said, taking Edward's hand.

Kevin frowned. "No, I can't stay, just wanted to make sure Ed was okay."

"He'll be coming to stay with me for a while when they release him," Alex told him, causing Kevin's frown to deepen.

"Oh. That's good I guess." He gave them a sickly smile. "Looks like I'll have the whole place to myself, then."

"Aren't you concerned about what might have happened to Troy?" Edward had to ask.

Kevin shrugged. "He's done this before. You saw what he's like on drugs. He can't seem to use any common sense—not that he has much of that to begin with anyway. He's a loser, and I'm not going to put up with him much longer. When he comes back I'm going to tell him to look for another apartment. You and me can share the one we have now, Ed."

"That's a bit cold, Kevin," Edward said. "He might be really sick, or— God knows what might have happened to him."

"You were the last one of us to see him. How did he seem to you?"

"He was with a bunch of guys and Herbie, a guy from the Rockin' Bar. I could tell he was already high and didn't want to listen to me."

"That's what I mean. You can't talk to him when he's using. He'll come back eventually. But I'm over him." He glanced at his watch. "Well, I gotta go. Got a hot date, though I have to admit"—he paused and winked at Alex—"not as hot as you."

Alex, who had remained quiet during Kevin's opinion of Troy, shook his head as the door closed behind Kevin. "Not much to choose between either of your roommates if you ask me. You're not considering getting a place with him, are you?"

"No way. I'll stay for the length of the lease then look around for something else."

"Well, we'll talk about that when the time comes." Alex leaned in to kiss Edward's cheek. "I hate to leave you, but I kinda left Lena in the lurch earlier. I should head over there and make sure she's okay. She, uh, has a similar problem to Troy."

"Oh, I understand. Will you come by tomorrow?"

"Of course. I'll be here to take you to my place. And maybe by then we'll know what's going on with Troy.

I have a feeling he just might have some information about what happened to you. Maybe Detective McLennan will have some news."

"About my car, at least. If Troy took it, he'd better return it." He sighed and let his head fall back on the pillow. "What's that old saying? 'No good deed goes unpunished.' Man, I know what it means now."

Alex stroked his cheek then kissed him gently. "Don't worry, I'll do some good deeds for you, soon as you're feeling better."

"Do 'em now," Edward whispered, wrapping an arm round Alex's neck to deepen their kiss.

"Can't," Alex said when they finally came up for air. "Someone might come in and catch us at it." They chuckled together then Alex stood and Edward was happy to see the obvious bulge behind his fly.

"You sure?" he asked, teasing as he ran his hand over Alex's crotch.

Alex growled. "You may look like an angel, but I'm beginning to know you better. Try to behave until I see you tomorrow." Then, after one more kiss, he was gone.

* * * *

Alex hadn't wanted to leave Edward, but he was also worried about Lena. He knew that giving in to her demands would solve nothing, but they had been friends for a long time, and he'd hated to hear her sound so distraught. After punching in the code that opened the gated entrance to her home, he drove up the long, curving driveway and parked under the porte-cochère. He noticed there was another car in front of his — a Jaguar.

Jeff's? he wondered as he climbed out of his BMW. *Thought he drove a Mercedes.*

Although he had a key, he rang the doorbell, just in case Lena was entertaining. Sophia, her secretary, answered and gave Alex a big smile.

"Is she busy?" he asked.

Sophia chuckled and rolled her eyes. "Ryan Hart's here. They're out by the pool having a drink. Go on through."

Wow, Jeff didn't waste any time arranging this little romantic meeting.

Alex walked into the luxurious house with its ankle-deep carpeting and oriental furnishings. Hank had bought the house for Lena as a wedding gift, and she'd had it decorated to her own ethnic taste. Lena's father, now deceased, had been a Chinese diplomat, her mother Eurasian. Lena had been raised in California but had always been fascinated with the art of her father's country.

Beyond the shimmering blue light cast by the pool water, he could see two shadowy figures sitting at the outside bar. For a moment he was hesitant to approach them. This, after all, was Jeff's solution to Lena's fragile psyche. And, who knew? He might just be right. Perhaps what Lena needed was a man in her life who could make her forget her sorrow and her need for artificial stimulants.

He loitered by the sliding-glass door, listening to the clink of ice in glasses and the soft murmur of conversation. *They seem to be getting along.* He took a step back into the living room.

"Alex, there you are!"

Lena's welcoming cry gave him no choice but to step onto the patio and walk the short distance to where she and Ryan Hart were seated. Hart rose and extended a hand as Alex approached.

"Alex, this is Ryan Hart," Lena exclaimed, weaving slightly on the bar stool. It was obvious she'd had a couple of whatever they were drinking. "Have you met before?"

"No, pleased to meet you." Alex shook the proffered hand and smiled at Hart whose grip was aggressive, his whitened teeth gleaming in his tanned face.

"So, you're the one I have to impress, huh?" Hart increased the pressure of his grip as if challenging Alex. "Lena tells me you're the best friend she's ever had."

Alex jerked his hand free from Hart's overly zealous grasp. "We've known each other a long time," he said, rounding the bar to give Lena a peck on the cheek.

"Pour yourself a drink."

"No thanks. I don't want to interrupt. Just wanted to make sure you were okay."

"How's your friend?" she asked, surprising him.

"He'll survive. I'm picking him up from the hospital tomorrow. He's going to stay with me for a few days while he recuperates."

"Really?" Lena arched a perfectly shaped eyebrow. "So, this is serious?"

"No, Lena. At least I wouldn't presume to say so at this early stage. He just needs somewhere to stay for a while. His roommates aren't the caring kind, and one of them is missing."

"Missing?" Ryan Hart laid his glass on the bar. "Sounds intriguing. Missing how?"

"We're not sure. The police are on it."

"Alex." Lena frowned at him. "What kind of people are you involved with? This doesn't sound like something that should concern you. You hardly know this man in the hospital."

"That's true, Lena, but it's my concern. It's not his fault his roommates are flakes."

"I get the feeling you're the nurturing kind, huh, Alex?" Hart was staring at him, a slight smirk on his lips.

Alex shrugged, but Lena answered for him. "Alex is the Good Samaritan to a fault," she said, placing a hand on his arm. "He's always been there for me — and Hank." Her eyes clouded and she gripped Alex's biceps tightly. "I don't know what I would have done…" Her voice trailed off to a whisper.

"Sweetie, you'd have been just fine." Alex put his arm around her shoulders and kissed her cheek. "I better go and leave you two to talk — about whatever it was I interrupted." He knew Lena would prefer that he stay. He already didn't like Ryan Hart, and couldn't see that this arranged match would work, but right now wasn't the time to voice that opinion. "I'll call you tomorrow." After giving Lena a quick hug, he looked at Hart. "Nice meeting you."

"Likewise," Hart drawled then walked with Alex to the sliding-glass doors. "Hey, I could use your help here," he said in a low voice. "Jeff thinks the publicity would be great for both our careers, and she seems to value your advice, so…"

Alex looked him straight in the eye. "I will always do what I think is best for Lena, but one thing you'll learn about her — if she doesn't want to do something, she won't. Goodnight." He left Hart standing there and strode quickly through the house to the front door. Sophia waylaid him just before he could leave.

"What d'you think of him?" she asked, a wry smile twisting her lips.

"He's an ass."

"We're on the same page, Alex." She opened the door for him. "G'night, Alex."

"G'night, Sophia."

* * * *

Alex glanced at his watch as he left. Almost nine. He wondered if he should stop by the Rockin' Bar. Somebody there might have heard about Troy's disappearance, or might even know where he was. Drugs could do terrible things to a person's mental state. Could be that Troy had crashed at some guy's apartment and was still unable to think or act coherently. Edward had said that Herbie had been at the party, had offered to drive Troy home. Maybe he was still shacked up at Herbie's place, although it seemed strange Herbie wouldn't let Kevin know Troy was with him.

Of course if Herbie had been in a similar state, anything was possible. He knew that only too well.

The Rockin' Bar was nowhere close to being as busy as the last time Alex was there, the night he'd met Edward. Gary, the regular bartender, was working and greeted Alex with his usual welcoming smile.

"Hey, handsome, where have you been hiding yourself?"

"Faraway places," Alex replied, grinning. He liked Gary's easy attitude and ready smile. He made a great bartender.

"What'll it be?"

"Just a tonic water with a squeeze of lemon."

"On the wagon, huh?"

"Not really, just not in the mood for anything stronger." He watched as Gary poured the tonic then ran a lemon wedge round the rim before squeezing a little of the juice into the glass. "You remember the last time I was here you introduced me to a guy from North Carolina. Edward?"

"Sure do. A cutie pie if ever there was one. You lose him or something?"

Alex chuckled. "No. Actually we've been seeing each other since then, but here's the thing—the other night he was in a kind of accident and I think Herbie—you know who I mean? Little guy with tattoos?"

"Who doesn't know Herbie?" Gary said, laughing. "He's over there in the corner singing the blues to anyone who'll listen. So is Ed okay?"

"He will be." Alex picked up his glass and pushed a ten toward Gary. "Thanks, I'll go over and help Herbie with his singing."

"Can't make it worse. From what I understand it's long and monotonous."

Alex wandered over to the far corner of the bar Gary had indicated. Herbie was sitting at a table, his head drooping onto his chest. No one was near him. It looked like everyone had tired of listening to him.

"Hi, Herbie." Alex sat down next to him.

Herbie raised his head slowly and regarded him through red-rimmed eyes. "Hi, yourself. Slumming tonight?"

"I've been here before, a couple of times. Just wanted to know if you had any idea where Troy Kendall might be. You offered to drive him home from a party last Saturday night, and he hasn't been seen since."

"Is that right?"

"Yes. Did you in fact drive Troy home?"

"Nope, never got the chance. He left with Edward and some other guy. The son of a bitch dumped me for them."

Alex ran this information through his mind. Edward, Troy and 'some other guy' all left together? But from what Edward had said he had no recollection of that happening.

"Edward was drugged, Herbie. Someone put a roofie in his drink." He paused to let Herbie absorb this, and, to his credit, the guy appeared to be dumbfounded.

"You're kidding, right?" His glazed expression began to clear. "But that might explain things…"

"What things?"

"Like it looked to me as if Ed was being carried out and Troy was pulling at them, like he was trying to stop them."

"You didn't go find out what was happening?"

"No, man, I was there to have a good time, not chase after some jerk who'd dumped me. I just figured, you know, Troy was pissed that Ed had hooked up with somebody else. Anyway they all got in a car—" Herbie stopped talking and to Alex it seemed as if he was trying to recall something more. "Things were a bit hazy at the time. Too much to drink I guess. I've felt shitty ever since that night. I've had hangovers before but this one's been a doozy."

Alex didn't ask why Herbie was in a bar with a drink in front of him if he was still hung-over. *Hair of the dog maybe?* "Can you remember anything else, Herbie? Troy is still missing so anything you can think of would be a big help. The police are investigating his disappearance—"

"The cops? Shit!"

"Well, yes. Edward was found lying on the side of the road and Troy has vanished. The police are looking at this as a crime. My concern is that if it's not resolved quickly, the FBI might get called in, as this involves drugs."

"I don't do drugs, man. Booze is enough for me, but there were drugs being thrown around all over the place that night. Troy was definitely on something." He closed his eyes for a moment then opened them wide and stared at Alex. "Yeah, now when I think about, there could have been some kind of struggle going on outside the car. Oh, man, I just thought Troy was high, and being a giant pain in the ass. Maybe he was trying to protect Ed. Shit." He fell silent, his expression morose.

"You don't know who this other guy was?" Alex asked.

"Oh yeah, it was the guy who was throwing the party. Walter something. Don't know his last name."

"Thanks, Herbie." Alex rose from the table. "You've been a big help." *Totally irresponsible, but maybe, just maybe you've given us enough to help the police investigation.* "Hey, by the way, I never did know your last name."

"It's Schenk."

"Good to know. Okay, thanks again. See you around."

Chapter Nine

As he headed for his car, Alex called the local police precinct and asked for Detective McLennan. He half expected to be told the detective wasn't there as he'd been on duty earlier in the day when he'd interviewed Edward, but he was put on hold and after a few moments, he heard a deep voice say, "McLennan, can I help you?"

"Yeah, hi, this is Alex Martinez, a friend of Edward Conway's. You remember we spoke at the hospital this morning?"

"Yes, what can I do for you?"

"Well, I was just talking with Herbie Schenk. He was at the same party as Edward and the missing roommate Troy Kendall. He said he saw Edward being taken out of the house by the owner and it looked like Troy was trying to prevent it."

"And this Herbie Schenk didn't do anything to stop what was happening?"

"No, I guess he was pretty drunk. He didn't seem to have much recollection at all of the incident until I started asking him questions. I must have triggered some kind of memory. He said he thought Troy was high and just fooling around, but once he really started thinking about it, he said it was more like a struggle to stop Edward being shoved into a car."

"Does he know the owner's name?"

"Walter—he didn't know the last name, but here's the thing, I think it might be Walter Jacobs."

"Why would you think that?"

"I work for the Scott Malone Agency. We do publicity for film celebrities and I attended a film shoot for one of our clients a few months ago. It was at Jacobs' house in the Hills. He's an interior designer for really wealthy people. I could be wrong, but the location and the first name struck me as maybe more than just a coincidence."

"Hmm...." There was a lengthy pause and Alex figured McLennan was wondering if this was a credible lead or something that might start him off on a wild goose chase. "I'll check it out tomorrow," the detective said finally.

"No word on Troy Kendall yet?" Alex asked.

"We have a possible lead, but I can't tell you more than that right now. Maybe tomorrow, if it checks out."

"I hope it does. They're releasing Edward tomorrow."

"Good to hear. You'll, uh, be visiting him no doubt?"

"He's staying with me until he's stronger. I don't think he'd get much aftercare from the other roommate."

McLennan chuckled dryly. "I think you're right about that. Well, thank you for the information, Mr. Martinez. We'll let you know if anything pans out. Goodnight."

"Goodnight, Detective."

Alex hung up and sat back in his car seat. He had to admit that he was more than a little curious about whether he was right or wrong about Walter Jacobs. He cast his mind back to the day when he'd accompanied Jeff Alderman, a young, rising TV star, and a photographic crew to Jacobs' house for the photo shoot. He remembered Jacobs as silver-haired, smoothly urbane in manner, with a little too much of the Southern charm oozing from every word. His persona didn't quite fit the image of him struggling with Troy and trying to push Edward into a car. But, of course, much stranger things had happened, and with booze and drugs on the menu, virtually anything was possible. He glanced at the digital clock on the dash.

Just gone ten… Is there really any point in driving up there now to snoop around? And what do I expect to find – Jacobs involved in some kind of drug orgy? It didn't seem likely, and if he remembered right, there were security gates at the end of the driveway, which would prevent him getting near the house. *I can't really go climbing over walls at this time of night. With my luck some neighbor might call the cops.*

His cell phone rang. Lena. He was tempted to let it go to voicemail, but maybe she needed something. "Hi, Lena."

"So what did you think?"

"About what?" he asked, teasing her.

"Ryan Hart, of course! Did he seem sincere to you?"

No. "As sincere as an egotistical movie actor can be, I suppose."

"Oh, I-I kind of liked him, Alex."

"You did? Well, that's all that matters, isn't it?"

"You don't approve." She sounded petulant. "He spoke rather warmly about you."

"I'm not going to marry him, no matter how much he likes me."

She giggled. "Oh, Alex, you're so funny. Hank always said you could make him laugh more than anyone else he knew." She fell silent, and Alex could almost see the tears welling in her eyes.

"Lena, sweetie," he said gently, "it really is time for you to move on and find some happiness. If not with Ryan Hart, then with *someone*. Someone who will take care of you and make you smile."

"You do that, Alex."

"Well..." He thought he'd better head off the maudlin direction Lena was taking their conversation in again. "I hate to break it to ya, honey, but I ain't the marryin' kind."

He smiled when he heard her giggle again. "Not with a lady anyway," she said.

"That's right. Now why don't you hit the hay, li'l darlin', and get some shuteye. I'll come visit tomorrow. Uh, in the afternoon," he added, remembering his first priority was getting Edward out of the hospital and over to his house.

Her sigh filled his ear. "Okay, I am kinda tired."

"Have Sophia make you some hot chocolate."

"Goodnight, Alex."

"G'night, sweetie."

* * * *

The following day

Mark McLennan stared down at the young man in the hospital bed for a few moments before trying to wake him. His roommate, Kevin Marshall, had called him cute, but Troy Kendall was more than that. Even with the cuts and bruises marring his face, McLennan could see there was a handsome man who would heal up very nicely indeed. The photograph Kevin Marshall had given didn't do Troy justice at all—the same photograph that McLennan had taken from his pocket and looked at several times over the last twenty-four hours.

He touched Troy's hand gently. "Mr. Troy Kendall?"

"Yeah, that's me, I think." Troy gazed back at him, his eyes slightly out of focus. "Hey, good-lookin', who are you?"

"Detective McLennan, LAPD. How are you feeling?"

"Like shit. That's what happens when you've been stuck in a hole for three days, I suppose."

"You're a very lucky man, Mr. Kendall. If those hikers hadn't heard you shouting for help, you might still be there."

"That supposed to make me feel better?"

McLennan pulled up a chair and sat by Troy's bed. "A lot of people have been worried about you, Mr. Kendall."

"Really? That makes a change. Who, for instance?"

"Your roommate, Edward Conway, for one. He's in this hospital too. Has been for the past three days."

"Is he okay?" For the first time, a glimmer of recollection and concern showed in Troy's expression.

"He'll be released this morning. So, tell me, what happened Saturday night. Tell me as much as you can remember."

Troy frowned. "It was that bastard Walter Jacobs. He had Garth, the bartender at the party, spike Ed's drink. I saw him do it, but I was a bit, uh, under the weather at the time, and I couldn't stop Ed from drinking it. At first, I had this goofy thought that it might lighten Ed up a bit. He's so uptight about so many things, you know? But then I saw him fall down and Walter go over and try to get him on his feet. I knew what he had in mind. I mean I was kinda out of it myself, but not so far gone I couldn't see what the s.o.b. was up to."

"So you tried to stop Jacobs?"

"Yeah." He squinted up at McLennan. "How d'you know that?"

"Your other friend, Herbert Schenk, gave this information to Alex Martinez, who called me last night. This morning I managed to speak directly to Mr. Schenk and he verified what he'd said."

"Herbert Schenk? Who the hell is that?"

McLennan sighed. "You might know him as Herbie. Tattoos?"

"Oh, yeah. He was going to drive me home, but then… Things happened."

"Right, and it's those *things* I want to hear about."

"I wish I could remember all of it."

"Tell me as much as you can."

"Where are you going?" Herbie yelled from behind him.

Troy wasn't sure why he was following Edward out of the room, but he did feel a little bad about letting him wander about on his own. He'd said he was leaving, but a lot could happen to a person in this place. He'd seen stuff – stuff he tried to forget in the cold light of day. Even now, as high as he was, he wanted to make sure Edward got to his car okay. Southern-fried was an uptight pain, but he'd been good enough to bring him here, and he didn't want to see anything bad happen to him.

There he is, talking to Walter Jacobs. Yeah, Ed is definitely Walter's type all right. *His gaze flitted over to where Garth was mixing a drink. He saw Garth's hand* hover over the rim for an instant, and knew what was happening.

"Hey..." He started forward. A wave of dizziness flooded his brain and he fell on his face. Hands grabbed at him, a voice, a braying laugh – the guy with the tattoos was helping him up. "Gotta stop Ed from drinking that..." Too late. He saw Edward throw the drink back. The tattooed guy hauled at his arms.

"Come on with me!"

"No – Gotta go help Ed."

"Son of a bitch!"

The hands released him and he lurched toward where Jacobs was now half carrying Edward outside.

"You dumping me?"

The angry cry didn't make any sense. Dumping who? Walter and Edward were standing at a car. Jacobs was fumbling with keys, while propping Edward up. Troy recognized it as Edward's car. He pushed Jacobs aside.

"What're you doing? Leave him alone."

With an angry snarl, Jacobs wrenched the car door open and threw Edward inside, then started to climb in after him. Troy grabbed his arm, trying to pull him back out. Jacobs turned the key, the car roared into life and started to back down the driveway. Troy ran with it. He pulled open the back door and jumped in.

"What the hell are you doing?" Jacobs yelled.

"What are you doing with my roommate?" Troy yelled back.

"Mind your own damned business. Now get out of this car." He braked hard and Troy's face collided with the back of Jacobs' head. "Dammit! Get out."

Troy saw stars and his nose throbbed. He fell back against the seat rest. "Where are you going?"

"How the hell would I know? I wasn't going any farther than the car until you interfered."

"What, you were going to rape him in the car? I saw Garth throw something into Ed's drink. The cops'll want to hear all about what you've been trying to do."

"Damn you!" The car flew backward through the gates out onto the street. Jacobs maneuvered it to the right and sped up the hill.

Troy was finding it harder to concentrate. His head spun, his stomach churned and he couldn't keep his eyes open. He became aware of a struggle in the front seats. Forcing himself to sit up, he saw Jacobs holding Edward by the arm while his roommate tried to open the car door.

"No, Ed…" His voice didn't sound like it belonged to him anymore. He reached out to grab Edward by the collar, but the car suddenly swerved and he was thrown back into the seat. A rush of air filled the interior, he heard a startled cry, Jacobs screaming "Jesus Christ!" then everything went black.

"That's all I remember." Troy gazed up at the detective, and wiped at the moisture that had gathered in his eyes. "The next thing I knew, I was lying on my back on top of rocks and hurting like a son of a bitch all over." McLennan handed him a tissue from a box near the bed. "Thanks. Sorry, I'm usually not the blubbery kind. Hard-hearted Hannah, Kevin calls me."

"It's okay. You've been through a really rough time. You're entitled to feel emotional."

"You're nice. You sure you're a cop?"

McLennan chuckled. "I'm sure, Mr. Kendall."

"Call me Troy. I mean, you're practically in bed with me."

McLennan's cheeks turned pink and Troy laughed then winced, holding his left side. "Ouch, that's from where I fell on a couple of big rocks. Sorry, didn't mean to embarrass you." He sighed and bit his lip. "I guess I kinda messed things up for Ed. Could be that jackass, Walter, only planned on giving him a blow job. He jumped out of the car, didn't he?"

McLennan nodded. "He was found lying on the road. His injuries aren't that serious—a lot of bruising, but fortunately nothing broken. However, he had been drugged as you thought. If you hadn't intervened, the outcome might have been much worse. You can't be sure what Walter Jacobs intended to do. Rohypnol is known as the 'date rape drug' for a reason."

"Jesus, that bastard."

"Right. Now we just have to find out how you ended up at the bottom of that gully in Wilderness Park."

"It had to have been Walter." Troy said, biting his lip. "But why would he do such a crazy thing?"

"My guess is he panicked. We'll know his reasoning soon enough. There's a warrant out for his arrest and a squad car is on its way over to his house even as we speak."

"He'll deny everything."

"A little hard to do, with witnesses to confirm his actions." McLennan rose from his seat. "Don't worry, he'll have his day in court. We'll need written statements from you, Edward Conway and, of course, Herbert Schenk."

"*The Illustrated Man*," Troy said with a chuckle.

"Oh, you read Ray Bradbury?"

"Used to when I was a kid."

McLennan gave him a wry smile. "You're still a kid, Troy. Just grow up and forget about drugs so you can grow old. No repeats of what happened Saturday night or I might have to arrest *you* next time."

"There won't be a next time, Detective. This was too close a call."

"Good. Keep thinking that way."

"Hey." Troy gave him a mischievous smile. "If you did arrest me…" He held out his hands as if in surrender. "Would you put handcuffs on me?"

"I might." McLennan smiled and took Troy's hand. He rubbed his thumb over Troy's wrist. "Seems a pity to mark this nice smooth skin, though."

"Wow, Detective, are you coming on to me? Is this even appropriate?"

"Absolutely not. Gonna report me?"

"Absolutely — unless there's a date lined up for when I get out of here."

"You got me." McLennan squeezed Troy's hand before releasing him. "I'll be in touch."

"You didn't tell me your first name."

"It's Mark."

"Suits you — strong, like you."

McLennan grinned. "Get some sleep, Troy. I'll be back later."

* * * *

Edward leaned on Alex as he led him into the house. He had to admit that no matter how hard he tried to convince himself he no longer hurt, every step was just a little bit of hell. His knees apparently had taken the brunt of his fall, and as Doctor Wingate told him, he was lucky the kneecaps weren't fractured. But oh boy, they hurt!

"The couch, or bed?" Alex asked as they entered the living room.

"Couch for now. I'd really like to sit."

"Couch it is." Alex lowered him gently onto the leather cushions, then gave him a quick peck on the cheek. "The good doctor says you should have painkillers only with food, so how about I make us a sandwich then you can have something to take that look of intense misery off your face."

"Sorry, but it does hurt like a son of a bitch."

"I'm sure. And don't say sorry. This is why you're here with me — to be waited on hand and foot. Nurse Ratched at your service." They laughed together. "So, what'll it be? I have ham and cheese, tuna salad, or pastrami."

"Anything will be better than what they served in the hospital," Edward said, grimacing at the memory of his last meal there. "I didn't know there were so many ways to screw up scrambled eggs."

"Tuna salad then?"

"Sounds good, Alex, thanks."

"Be right back."

Edward sank back into the softness of the couch pillows and, sighing softly, closed his eyes. Detective McLennan had come to see him before he was released and related what Troy had told him. He'd wanted to go visit Troy and thank him and find out if he was feeling better, but the nurses had told him Troy was exhausted and sleeping soundly. Alex had suggested they call him later and Edward had agreed that was probably best.

He was still in some shock from what McLennan and Alex had told him. That Walter Jacobs was the one who'd drugged him, and that Troy had tried to prevent the whole thing. He felt bad about blaming Troy for maybe drugging him, and even worse that the guy had been thrown into a gully and left for dead, presumably by Jacobs.

The man must have been freaked when I jumped out of the car and Troy threatened him with the police. But what a cold-blooded thing to do to Troy — leave him out in the wilderness to die. Thank God the two men hiking nearby heard his cry for help, weak though it must have been.

Fortunately, apart from cuts and bruises sustained from being rolled over rocks into the gully, Troy's most severe problem had been dehydration. The paramedics who arrived at the scene had immediately put him on a portable IV until he was admitted into Emergency and they could take over.

Wow, what a way to end a Saturday night party.

He opened his eyes at the sound of Alex coming back into the living room. He carried in a tray with their tuna salad sandwiches, two large glasses of water and Edward's prescribed pain meds. The tray had folding legs that he opened and placed over Edward's legs.

"There." He grinned at Edward. "Service with a smile, sir. If there's anything lacking in my style of servitude, you may bring out the whip—after you've eaten, of course."

Edward chuckled. "Didn't know you were into whips."

"I'm not, so don't go getting any ideas." He took his sandwich and settled on the couch next to Edward. "Eat now. We have to build up your strength, get you well again."

Edward ate with relish. "Delicious," he mumbled through a mouthful.

"There's more."

"No, this is good, thanks. Maybe later."

"Should I pick up some of your things from the apartment?" Alex asked. "You can use anything of mine until you're ready to go back to work, if you like, but is there any personal stuff you need?"

Edward thought for a moment. "Not really. My overnight bag should still be here from when I was going to stay over before all this happened. It's got my toothbrush and stuff."

"Right, I put it in the guest bathroom. So you're all set for a few days, now take your painkillers." He opened the small bottle and handed Edward two pills. "Then off to bed with you."

Edward swallowed them down with water, gratefully. His knees ached with a painful, insistent throb. "Bed sounds good, if I can just stand up."

"No need." Alex set the tray aside. He slipped one arm under Edward's thighs, the other supporting his shoulders, and he lifted Edward off the couch with apparent ease. Edward clung to him as he was carried across the living room and into the guest room.

"And they say there are no such things as knights in shining armor," he said, nuzzling Alex's ear.

"Not so shiny," Alex replied, laying Edward gently onto the bed then planting a kiss on his forehead. "I'll bring a couple of icepacks for your knees. Be right back."

Edward could feel sleep tugging at his eyelids. The bed was so comfortable, the pillow soft and welcoming. It would be so easy to drift off. The sharp ring of his cell phone Alex had placed on the nightstand beside him brought him abruptly back to reality. He squinted at the caller ID screen.

Troy. "Hey, Troy."

"You didn't come see me before you left."

"I wanted to, but the nurse said you couldn't be disturbed. How're you feeling?"

"Better than I did when they found me yesterday. How about you?"

"Getting there. I'm staying with Alex for a few days."

"Lucky you. You've got a keeper there."

"I hope so. Listen, Troy, I want to thank you for what you did, what you tried to do. When Alex and Detective McLennan told me, I just couldn't believe it."

He heard a weak chuckle then Troy said, "Yeah, kinda out of character for me, huh?"

"No, I didn't mean that. I meant what Walter Jacobs did to you. The guy must be some kind of psycho."

"He's as mean as a snake. He better run when I get out of here. I intend to pull that dyed hair of his out by the roots."

"I think he'll be locked up by then. Probably is right now. Has Kevin been to see you?"

"Yeah, he stopped by for a few minutes, full of I told you sos." Troy sighed heavily. "Ah do declah, Miss Southern-fried, I might have to find me a new mansion to call mah own."

Edward laughed. "You do that so well. But don't do anything hasty. You and Kevin have been friends for a long time."

"Yeah, guess so. Better the devil and all that jazz." He was silent for a few seconds then he said, "I guess we were both lucky to have survived this, huh? When I woke up in that hole, it was dark. I couldn't figure out where I was, and, Ed, I have to tell you I was scared shitless. When daylight came all I could see were rock walls. I couldn't get out. I thought I'd really had it, and all I could think of was just what a waste I'd made of my life."

Edward could hear the sadness in Troy's voice and he wished he could be there to give him more comfort than he could over the phone. "I don't want to join in with the I told you sos, Troy, but please, please tell me you're going to give up the drugs."

"Don't worry, I've learned my lesson. Lying in the dark, thinking I was going to die, made me realize how much I want to live—and not getting wasted is the way to start. Hey, by the way, what d'you think of that hunky detective who's handling the case? I'd like for him to handle me, for sure."

Edward chuckled. "You're sounding better already. It's pretty obvious what you think of him."

"He was flirting with me the whole time."

"Really? Isn't that—?"

"Inappropriate? I kinda started it. I could tell he was interested but he probably wouldn't have gone there without some encouragement from *moi*, so I coerced him into agreeing to go on a date with me when I get out of the hospital!"

"Troy, you are too much."

"I know. Darn, but I'm getting woozy again. Must be the drugs. The hospital ones I mean."

"Okay, get some sleep. We'll talk again soon. Bye."

"Bye, Southern friend."

"Don't you mean Southern-fried?"

"Not this time. Bye."

"That was Troy," Edward told Alex as he returned with the icepacks.

"How is he?" Alex pulled back the comforter to expose Edward's legs. "These will be chilly, but they'll bring down the swelling."

Edward shivered as Alex applied the ice-cold compresses to his knees. "He sounded pretty good, considering what he's been through, and, Alex, he also sounded like a much nicer person."

"He might have had an epiphany lying there in that awful place."

"He said it made him realize how much he wanted to live. And guess what? He thinks Detective McLennan is hot. "

Alex shrugged. "He's a good-looking dude." He chuckled. "Troy and a cop—now that's something I didn't see coming!"

Chapter Ten

The following day Edward woke to the sound of soft music and the delicious aroma of freshly brewed coffee. He sat up, rubbed his eyes, then swung his legs over the edge of the bed. Carefully, he stood upright, trying to gage whether or not his knees were up to supporting him on the short walk to the bathroom. He took a couple of tentative steps.

Feels better... Much better. He crossed the carpeted floor to the bathroom without any trouble and once he'd relieved himself and washed his hands and face, he slipped on the robe Alex had left for him and made his way to the kitchen. Alex greeted him with a big smile. He wore black sweatpants and a blue T-shirt, and his thick hair was still tousled from his pillow. *He is stunning*, Edward thought.

"Look at you," Alex said. He delivered a hot kiss to Edward's lips then stepped back and surveyed his face critically. "Bruises are already fading. How are your knees?"

"Better. The ice packs you insisted I keep using really helped."

"Hmm, let me take a look." He knelt in front of Edward and opened the robe. "Yeah, the swelling has gone down quite a bit." He ran his hands up the insides of Edward's thighs until his fingers touched the underside of Edward's balls. He stroked them gently and Edward shivered from the exquisite sensation that coursed through him.

"And I'm being crass," Alex said, standing. "Taking advantage of you the way I did there. Come sit, and I'll pour you some coffee." He put an arm round Edward's waist and guided him over to the couch. "Black or white?"

"Uh…" Edward had to clear his throat before he could answer. "White with sugar, please." Alex's erotic touch was having a lasting effect on his senses, never mind his cock, which had hardened perceptibly. "I don't mind you taking advantage of me, you know."

"I know, but I shouldn't in your weakened state," Alex said firmly, from behind the kitchen counter. "Of course, that's not to say I won't take advantage of you when you're feeling A-okay."

"Then I promise to hurry the healing process." Edward smiled at Alex as he delivered their coffee. "Just being here with you is making me feel much better." Their eyes met and Edward felt a thrill ripple down his spine as he caught the intensity in Alex's dark gaze.

"God, but you're making it very hard for me — pardon the pun — to keep my hands off you." There was an undeniable tension in Alex's tone. He traced the line of Edward's jaw with his fingertips. "But…" He withdrew his hand and sat back a little. "Until you're a hundred percent better, you're in no-man's-land."

"Damn," Edward muttered and they both laughed.

Alex said, "I promise the wait will be worth it."

"I know it will."

The sound of the doorbell ringing had them exchanging quizzical glances. "Early for callers," Alex said, "and Blanca has her own key." He got up and hurried to the door. Edward could hear him talking with someone then he reappeared with Detective McLennan in tow.

"Good morning, Mr. Conway." The detective gave Edward a stiff nod. "You look a lot better today."

"Thanks, and please call me Edward."

"Would you like a coffee?" Alex asked.

"No, thanks."

"I'm guessing you have some news for us. Why don't you sit and relax and join us for coffee? You're allowed that even on duty, aren't you?"

McLennan managed a smile that softened his normally stern features. "As a matter of fact, I've been up all night getting a confession out of Walter Jacobs. Coffee does sound good right about now."

"Take a seat while I get it for you. Black or white?"

"Black's good." McLennan sat opposite Edward and stretched out his long legs.

"You look tired," Edward said. "Was Walter Jacobs denying the whole thing?"

"In the beginning, yeah. We had a stroke of luck when the police officers went over to his house with a search warrant and the guy you said was the bartender, a Garth Browning, was there with him. The officers searched the premises and, in the garage, they found a car that coincided with the description you gave of your vehicle. Browning caved right away, saying he didn't want to get involved in any drug charges."

"But he was the one who put the roofie in my drink!" Edward exclaimed.

"He denies all of it, of course, but Tr—uh, Mr. Kendall was witness to it." He looked up as Alex delivered his coffee. "Thanks." He took a sip. "Mmm, lot better than the muck we have at the station. So, anyway," he continued as Alex sat down next to Edward, "my guys took them both in for questioning, and it was obvious from the get-go they were in it up to their necks. Browning was no kind of alibi for Jacobs, just spilling his guts any which way, trying to get out of being associated with him."

He took another sip of his coffee then chuckled. "If Jacobs could've killed him with a look, Browning would be a dead man. Jacobs called for his attorney but when Garth Browning said Jacobs told him to drug your drink, then also confessed he saw Mr. Kendall try to stop Jacobs shoving you into your car, they had no choice but to ask for a deal. They'll both go to jail, but most likely for a few years less than if they hadn't confessed. The attorney knew a jury wouldn't be lenient on hearing they had drugged you, and Jacobs had thrown Mr. Kendall into a gully and left him to die."

Edward shuddered. "Did he say why he did that to Troy?"

McLennan nodded. "He said he wasn't thinking straight. After you jumped out of the car, Mr. Kendall told him he was going to call the police, but then he passed out and Jacobs panicked, knowing he couldn't let him talk. He was desperate, afraid of being found with an unconscious man in the back of a car that didn't belong to him. He said he considered driving back to the house and getting Garth Browning to dispose of the evidence."

"You mean dispose of Troy?" Edward gaped at the detective.

"Well, I think he was just trying to implicate Browning even more, suggest that Browning might be capable of doing such a thing, or maybe even had done something similar before. Anyway, Browning shrieked like a banshee when Jacobs implied it, blathering at the top of his voice that he hadn't even wanted to bartend that night, and that Jacobs was a big fat liar. It wasn't pretty." McLennan paused to drink the rest of his coffee.

"Have you spoken to Troy, told him all this?" Alex asked.

"Not yet. I'll be heading over to the hospital after I leave here."

"So, there won't be a trial?"

"As they've confessed, no. They'll be held until sentencing. Save the taxpayers some money, at least."

"I'm kinda glad," Edward said. "I really wasn't ecstatic about having to appear in court as a witness."

McLennan stood and held out his hand to Edward. "Glad to see you looking much better, Mr.... uh, *Edward*. I'll be in touch."

"Thanks." Edward shook the detective's strong hand. "When you see Troy — and by the way he spoke very highly of you, Detective — give him our best and tell him we'll be in to see him soon."

"Uh, yeah, I will. He'll, uh, he'll be glad to hear that."

He turned to go and Edward smiled. The detective was blushing all the way to the backs of his ears.

* * * *

Alex checked his cell phone messages after seeing McLennan out. There were several from Lena. *Better call her…*

"Hey, Edward, I have to return a few calls. Won't be long." *I hope.*

"Okay." Edward picked up the TV remote. "I'll watch the news."

"Good. I'll be right back." He went into his bedroom and punched in Lena's number. Maybe it wouldn't be anything too drastic. If it was, Sophia would've called too.

"Hi, Lena," he said when she answered. "Not too early, am I?"

"No, but where have you been?" She sounded vaguely put out, but not overly upset. "I thought you were going to call me last night."

"Yeah, sorry, I got kind of involved getting Edward out of hospital and, you know, things to do," he said, knowing it sounded lame.

"Well, I wanted you to be the first to know, but now it's probably too late. Jeff has been calling all the major news channels to make the announcement that Ryan and I are officially 'a couple'."

"A couple? What does that mean — you eloped, or something?"

Lena giggled. "No, silly, it's just the build-up to us being seen around town — dating, taking a trip together, you know, the usual fluff."

Alex wasn't sure how he felt about this development, but Lena appeared to be okay with it. His momentary silence had her asking, "Are you that surprised, Alex? You're the one who said I should move on."

"No, no. Not surprised. As long as you're sure this is what you want. Will marriage be the end result or have you not got that far?"

"Well, of course Jeff wants that possibility bandied about, but I want to take my time on that. Maybe wait a week or two before we get engaged."

That's taking your time? "So you're okay with Ryan Hart? You like him?"

"We understand one another, Alex. He's kinda funny, makes me laugh like you do. He's not the greatest kisser. Not bad, but there's room for improvement. I can handle it."

Oh, Lena. At least she didn't say 'not like Hank could kiss'. "If you're sure."

"Alex, he's the only guy Jeff's come up with that I can remotely stand. You won't marry me." She injected a light laugh before continuing. "So, what's a girl to do? Anyway, I was hoping to see you today but Jeff's arranged a press conference for Ryan and me, then I have to get together with Will about finishing the movie with him."

"Looks like you'll be busy for a while then," Alex said.

"Never too busy for you, darling. You'll always be my best friend."

Until Jeff and Ryan Hart put a stop to it. "Okay, I'll call you tomorrow."

"Oh, how's your friend — Edward, is it?"

"Right, Edward. He's getting there, and the good news is his missing roommate's been found — a little beaten up, but he'll survive. The men who did this have been arrested, so it's all good."

"Alex, are you sure you want to be involved with someone like this? It all sounds so —"

"Totally sure, Lena." He cut her off before she could say something he might find it hard to forgive her for. "I'll tell you the whole story one day. Better let you go so you can get ready for your press meeting."

"Oh, all right, Alex. Love you."

"Love you too."

Sighing, he ended the call and pocketed his cell. He wished he could be happier about this latest situation in Lena's life. He found it surprising she'd rolled over so easily with Jeff's demands. Maybe he'd misjudged Ryan Hart.

Nope, don't think I did.

He went back into the living room and slumped onto the couch next to Edward.

"What's wrong?" Edward turned off the TV and looked at him with concern. "Bad news?"

"Not really. My friend Lena is dating Ryan Hart."

"Ryan Hart, the movie star?"

"The one and the same."

"But you don't think it's a good idea?"

Alex groaned. "It really doesn't matter what I think, Edward. Soon there will be rumors of a Hollywood wedding between two major stars that will set the TV news media agog for weeks, boost the happy couple's careers, give the tabloids enough fodder for months — Lena and Ryan are engaged, they've called it off, it's on again, wedding bells are ringing, the honeymoon was a disaster, divorce imminent, Lena and Ryan deny marital problems —"

"Oh, wow." Edward stared at him and frowned. "I didn't know you were such a cynic."

"I've been around this business for too long I guess." He took Edward's hand. "Sorry, didn't mean to vent like that. It's just that Lena is a fragile soul and her agent is pushing her into this affair with Hart, who I don't think is a very nice guy. My fault too, I guess. I kept telling her to move on, find someone to make her happy. I just didn't think she'd go for this kind of arrangement."

"You mean her agent tells her who she should date, or even marry?"

Alex nodded. "It's not that unusual. Publicity love affairs are good press while they last, and some actually do end in a happy marriage."

"Arranged marriages," Edward murmured. "Who knew? I thought that kind of thing only happened in countries like India."

"Well, at least here, they do have the option of backing out if they think they're not at all compatible. Anyway..." He kissed the back of Edward's hand then got up. "I'm neglecting my caregiver duties, I haven't prepared your breakfast yet."

"Oh, don't bother with that. I don't eat a whole breakfast, just coffee and a Danish maybe."

"Hey, breakfast is the most important meal of the day, and while you're here you will have breakfast." Alex gave him a 'no argument' look and strode off to the kitchen. *It'll do me good to keep busy.* He opened the fridge and pulled out a box of eggs.

"You think we could go over and visit Troy today?" Edward asked.

"If you feel up to it. I have to admit I'm kinda interested to see this new and improved Troy myself."

"It is sort of hard to believe, but if it hadn't been for him, God knows what would've happened."

* * * *

After their breakfast at the kitchen counter, of scrambled eggs, sausage and toast, Edward announced he had to shower. "You can join me if you like," he said, giving Alex what he hoped was a sly, inviting smile. "My arms are still a bit stiff — makes it hard to reach my back."

"Hmm..." Alex appeared to be giving the matter serious thought. "Well, you do have a point, and I haven't showered yet, so — you're on. But..." He wagged a finger at Edward. "Don't expect any shenanigans, young man. You're not quite ready for that yet."

That's what you think. Edward gave him a sunny smile. "Whatever you say, O master." He was pretty sure that when they were both in such close proximity in the shower, he'd be able to change Alex's supposed steely resolve to keep his hands to himself. *After all, he is going to scrub my back...*

"Come on then." Alex took Edward's hand and helped him off the bar stool. "Would you like me to carry you again?"

"I think I'm okay." He was more than okay, but he slipped an arm around Alex's waist as if to steady himself. Alex reciprocated by wrapping an arm around Edward.

"We'll use my shower," Alex said. "There's more room to maneuver."

Edward frowned. *That's right, Alex's shower is huge. Damn.* He didn't want more room. He wanted Alex's body, slick with soapy water, pressed up against him with no 'room to maneuver' whatsoever. Well, he'd just have to be a bit more aggressive. Once he got Alex hard, that would be the end of his silly resolve.

In the bathroom, a marble-tiled affair with a sunken shower lined with the same tile, Alex turned on the water then quickly discarded his pants and T-shirt. Edward gasped at the beauty of Alex's body, the smoothly defined musculature of his chest and torso, and the slimness of his hips. He found it hard to tear his gaze from the sight of Alex's cock, impressive even in its now flaccid state. Something he hoped to alter in the next few minutes.

"Robe?" Alex was looking at him quizzically. "You need to take it off, Edward."

"Oh, right," he mumbled, undoing the belt and slipping the soft material from his shoulders. Alex continued to stare at him, his eyes darkening with undisguised lust. *Yes...*

They stepped under the hot spray. Alex grabbed a sponge and squeezed a liberal amount of body wash onto it. "Turn around." His voice was decidedly husky, then he proceeded to wash Edward's back, keeping an annoying distance between himself and Edward. When Edward felt the sponge pass over the base of his spine, he stuck out his butt, pressing against Alex's hand. The sponge slipped from Alex's grasp and landed with a plop onto the shower floor.

"Damn," Alex exclaimed, but before he could bend down to pick it up, Edward gripped his hand and forced his fingers into the cleft between his butt cheeks. "Edward," Alex muttered in warning, but it was half-hearted at best and did nothing to deter Edward from his mission. He turned to face Alex, wrapped his arms around him and kissed him with a passion he knew Alex wouldn't resist. It was obvious from the very hard flesh prodding Edward's thigh that he'd succeeded in breaking down Alex's resolve. So far so good, but Alex might just pull himself together and push Edward away. He couldn't let that happen.

He reached for Alex's erection and began to massage it, gently at first, then as a moan escaped Alex's throat, with sure, firm strokes. He wanted to get down on his knees and take Alex's cock in his mouth, but he knew that would be foolish and something that Alex wouldn't allow. He'd pull back immediately and stop him from risking even more pain. But this was good enough for now. He'd wanted to feel Alex's hard body pressed against his, wanted those rapturous kisses that took him to heights of ecstasy he'd never known existed before meeting Alex.

"This won't do," Alex said, his lips not leaving Edward's.

"What?" *No, don't make me stop, not now, not yet...*

"Finish showering. There's a bed out there that's a helluva lot more comfortable for what you've got in mind."

Edward figured he'd never showered and dried off as fast in all his life, but then there had never been anything quite so tempting at the end of any shower he'd had previously. The promise of sex with Alex was enough to make him almost race out of the bathroom, until his knees reminded him to take it easy.

"Uh-huh," Alex said, seeing him wince. "Maybe this isn't such a good idea."

"It's a great idea! C'mon, Alex, don't renege on me now. You'll have the blue balls from hell if you don't let me take care of you."

Alex chuckled and kissed Edward's nose. "Who could resist such a romantic invitation?" He patted Edward's bottom. "Okay, but the slightest hint of pain and we stop."

Edward nodded. *There isn't an agony in the universe that would make me tell you to stop...*

He got on the bed and lay back expectantly as Alex stood over him, stroking himself while he gazed down at Edward, his eyes filled with a hunger that sent a frisson of pure lust zinging through Edward's blood. Alex climbed onto the bed and took Edward gently into his arms. Edward could tell he was holding back for fear of hurting him, his kisses on Edward's lips and skin more tentative than erotic.

Edward let out a needy whimper and pushed himself hard into Alex's embrace. "I won't break," he whispered. Alex skimmed his lips over Edward's chest, teasing each nipple, lightly at first, then as Edward writhed against him, he used his teeth to bring each tiny nub to a tingling peak, sending electrifying jolts all the way to Edward's straining erection.

Alex kissed his way down Edward's torso, lingering over each bruise as if he could heal them with his touch. He dipped his tongue into Edward's navel before following the blond treasure trail leading to Edward's hard cock, the glistening tip an invitation Alex couldn't resist.

He grasped the throbbing flesh in one hand and licked the copious pre-cum oozing from the slit, relishing the slightly salty taste. Encouraged by Edward's low, throaty moans, he slid his lips down the hot, rigid length, taking it all the way to the shower-sweet muskiness of Edward's pubic hair at the root. He loved the feel of the hard, smooth flesh that seemed to fit so well inside his mouth and throat. As he sucked, his movements slow and deliberate, he cupped Edward's balls in his free hand, massaging them gently, feeling them tighten in his palm.

He felt Edward's fingers rake his hair, heard his muttered entreaty, "Let me take care of you, too…"

He shifted his body so that his cock was in reach of Edward's mouth and he shuddered with ecstasy as he felt soft lips enclose his throbbing erection and a demanding tongue lick its way up and down the length of his thick shaft. Alex's senses went on overload. He vowed to be careful handling Edward so as not to cause him any more pain, but right then all he could see, smell and taste was this beautiful man who, in such a short time, had begun to mean so much to him.

He wasn't going to fuck him, not this time — it would be too much for Edward to bear in his present state. There were other ways to bring him pleasure. He paused to lubricate his middle finger with his spit, then pushed it into the cleft between Edward's round butt cheeks and circled the tight pucker he found there. He probed gently at first, then as Edward writhed against him he slipped his finger far enough in to stroke Edward's prostate. When he took Edward's cock back into his mouth he was rewarded by a spurt of pre-cum, the salty tang coating his taste buds. Edward moaned, and his erection pulsed in Alex's mouth. His own climax was imminent — he knew he couldn't hold out much longer. As Edward orgasmed with a muffled cry, flooding Alex's mouth with his cum, Alex steeled himself to teeter on the knife edge of ecstasy for a few moments more before succumbing to the now unstoppable rush of liquid heat that spread from the base of his spine into his balls. He came in long shuddering spasms that racked his body and left him boneless and sweating.

Waiting only to feel Edward's erection soften he positioned himself alongside Edward and held him gently. "Are you all right?" he asked softly. "No pain?"

"Only the pain of not having you in my mouth."

Alex chuckled and pressed his lips to Edward's. Edward opened to him and their tongues tangled to share the taste of each other's cum.

"You're amazing," Alex whispered.

"If I'm amazing, there isn't a word great enough to describe you." Edward rested his head on Alex's chest. "Maybe super-amazing…"

* * * *

Later they drove to the hospital to visit Troy. When they entered the room Troy seemed to be asleep and Edward marveled at how young and defenseless he seemed in repose, so different from the smart-mouth Edward knew him to be. His face was marred by yellowing bruises, his forehead sported a large Band-Aid covering the stitches Doctor Wingate had told them Troy had needed on admittance.

"He doesn't look too bad," Edward whispered to Alex.

"I look like shit," Troy opened his eyes and grinned up at them. "Doesn't seem to turn Mark off, though."

"Mark?"

"Detective McLennan to you. He was here earlier giving me the lowdown on that fucker Walter Jacobs and that pig Garth whatshisname. Man, I'd like to—" He bit his lip suddenly. "No, I have to control my anger issues. Mark says I mustn't waste negative energy on jerks like them." He rolled his eyes, his grin returning. "I know, doesn't sound like me at all. So how're you, Southern-fried?"

"Oh, back to that I see," Edward said wryly.

"But now it's said with affection." He reached out and took Edward's hand. "You and me, we went through shit together, didn't we? But we came out the other side, and I hope you won't hold all those crappy things I've said to you against me."

Edward sat on the edge of the bed. "No, of course not. If it hadn't been for you, I might have been a lot worse off. Who knows what Jacobs was capable of."

"Right, he's a complete freak. So…" He smiled at Alex and winked. "Are you two *together*, together now?"

"Uh…" Alex gave Edward a quick glance before answering. "We're, uh, getting to know each other."

"I think you are totally into one another—in more ways than one."

"Hey." Edward frowned at Troy. "I thought you were a changed man—no more snark and smartass comments."

"Oh now, you ask too much of me!" Troy laughed and squeezed Edward's hand. "But…" His expression sobered and he added, "I want us to be friends, real friends, the kind you can count on when you have to. Mark says you were really concerned for me, and I— Shit, I'm not gonna cry, am I? It's just that I've never had anyone really care about me—at least not that they ever told me." He swiped at his eyes with his free hand while still holding onto Edward's. "Or maybe I was just too toasted all the time to hear what was being said."

Edward leaned down and did something he never could have imagined himself doing—he kissed Troy on the cheek. "Yes, Alex and I care for you, Troy, and…" He smiled into his roommate's eyes. "I think you might have a big and brave detective who also, given the chance, will care for you—in more ways than one."

Behind him, Alex chuckled. "Now who's a smartass?"

"Just joining the club."

A knock at the door had them all turning expectantly. Detective Mark McLennan stood hesitantly in the doorway. "Sorry, didn't know you'd have company," he said, biting his lower lip and looking slightly uncomfortable.

"Come on in," Troy said. Edward got up off the bed and moved over to stand beside Alex. "You have some more news of those two scumbags? They gonna get life in prison?"

"Not yet." He nodded at Edward and Alex then directed his gaze at Troy. "Sentencing's scheduled for next week. With the plea bargain I'd guess Jacobs will serve fifteen to twenty years." He paused for a moment then said, "I, uh, just spoke with your doctor. He told me you should be out of here in the next couple of days."

"Great." Troy flashed him a mischievous smile. "You haven't forgotten what that means, right?"

McLennan glanced at Edward and Alex, a ghost of a smile on his lips. "I'm not following you, Mr. Kendall," he said, looking back at Troy. "What is it I may have forgotten?"

"I think we should go," Alex whispered, nudging Edward.

Edward would like to have stayed to see the interplay between Troy and the detective, but Alex was right—they should go and leave Troy to get on with his seduction. After quick goodbyes and a promise to visit Troy the next day, they left, Edward closing the door slowly enough so he could just catch a glimpse of Detective McLennan bending down to kiss Troy on the lips.

* * * *

When they got back to Alex's house, he checked his text and voicemail on his cell. Two messages from Scott, but none from Lena. Strange, he mused — usually not a day went by without him hearing from her in one form or another. The press conference, then Jeff and Ryan Hart most likely were keeping her busy.

"How're you feeling?" he asked Edward, putting his cell in his pocket. He'd call Scott later.

"Good, thanks." Edward sounded tired but gave him a bright smile.

"Go lie down on the couch and I'll make us some tea or coffee. Which would you like?"

"Tea would be great, thanks." Edward sank down onto the couch and Alex could feel his eyes on him as he stood behind the kitchen counter filling the kettle with water.

"Can I ask you something?"

Alex nodded. "Sure, ask me anything you want."

"When you gave me the keys last Saturday, I didn't exactly go snooping but I did look at the photographs on the bookshelf over there. There's one of the friend you mentioned that night when we were in the pizza parlor — Hank. Only I didn't realize it was Hank Bartell, the movie star. I'm really sorry for your loss, Alex. I intended to tell you that, then all this mess happened." He paused for a moment then he said, "Anyway, what I wanted to ask, and please, if you think it's none of my business, or if you don't want to talk about it I'll understand, but were you and Hank, uh…?"

"Lovers?" Alex smiled. He flipped on the switch for the electric kettle then walked over to the couch and sat down by Edward. "Yes, Hank and I were lovers for over five years."

"How did you meet him?"

"We met in a bar, but it turned out we were both attending the same drama school. How we hadn't noticed each other before was a surprise to both of us. Two weeks after we met, we were living together."

"You went to drama school? How come you're not an actor too?" Edward asked.

Alex laughed. "Good question. I left after the first year. We'd done some plays, and I already had the idea that I wasn't very good. Then, after one production when a critic actually singled me out by saying I was more wooden than the spear I carried, I decided an actor's life was not for me.

"Hank didn't want me to quit, but I had already been scouting around for a real job and got lucky when Scott hired me as a trainee. I guess I made the grade as I'm still there. Hank, as you know, went on to become a major movie star. Those stellar looks of his just lit up the screen. He'd be the first to tell you he wasn't the greatest actor, but there was something about his persona, something intrinsically different about him, even more than his good looks. He was box office magic, without a doubt."

He fell silent—his mind filled with images of Hank's beautiful, smiling face. There was a time when talking about Hank or thinking about their life together would bring tears to his eyes, and he was gratified that this time, telling Edward, he remained in quiet control of his emotions.

"You loved him very much," Edward said softly, taking Alex's hand.

"Yes, and thankfully he loved me too. Even though we knew that a homosexual love affair was anathema to a Hollywood career, we were young and too damned besotted with each other to really worry about all that. Then, of course, reality came crashing in, in the form of sneaky rumors about Hank's secret love life, his love-nest orgies, his secret hideaway, crap like that. He was just another star on the 'gay list' the tabloids love to speculate about, but his agent and the producers of the movie he was making at the time, panicked—big time.

"'You have to be seen with women,' they yelled. 'Get married!' Hank kinda laughed at them to begin with, then they set him up with Lena. They'd worked together on a movie and the three of us had become friends. But they wanted me out of the picture and more or less told me I would ruin Hank's career if we continued to live together. 'You guys can't be seen together so much, even with Lena between you,' they told Hank. He was madder than a hornet, but in the end I made the decision to back off, for the sake of his reputation."

The strident whistling of the tea kettle startled them both, and Alex gave a half laugh. "Saved by the whistle," he said jokingly. "I'll be right back."

Edward sat quietly digesting what Alex had told him. The love Alex and Hank had shared seemed to him to be the perfect love story, one that in a perfect world would still be as vibrant as the day they met. Alex had said he'd backed off to save Hank's career— a sacrifice that in the end couldn't stop the tragedy of Hank's death.

God, why do people have to meddle in other's lives? Why is it so important that the face up on a screen must belong to the ideal of the perfect man, or woman?

Alex had seemed in control of his feelings as he told the story of his lost love, but it had to cut deep, especially in the way it had ended. He looked up as Alex came back carrying two mugs of tea.

"Careful, it's hot," he said, setting the mug on the coffee table.

"Thanks," Edward murmured. He waited until Alex had put down his own mug, then he slipped his arms around Alex and held him. "I am so sorry. This must have been horrendous for you. For both of you."

Alex stroked Edward's hair. "It was pretty devastating, but after we talked we knew we had to make the best of it. I couldn't let Hank's career go up in smoke because of me, even though he said he'd tell the producers to go to hell. I just couldn't let him do that. It would have been the end of everything for him. Yeah, we would have been happy in a cottage by the sea, probably..." He laughed a little. "But I loved him too much to let him do it. It was his whole life."

"But *you* were his life too."

"Right, but there was more than just the two of us involved. When a star reaches his or her zenith, a lot of people depend on them for their livelihoods. Hank knew this as well as I did. We thought in the beginning that if I moved out, and he was seen dating Lena, we could get together whenever we wanted to. Lena knew the score, and was fine with it—or so I thought—but then came the pressure for them to marry." He gently disengaged himself from Edward's arms. "Here, drink some tea before it gets cold."

They sipped their tea in silence for a few moments then Edward asked, "How did you feel about them getting married?"

"I thought I was going to be okay with it, then Lena laid her bombshell on me. She told me she was in love with Hank and wanted their marriage to be real. I knew at that point I had to step back. I talked with my boss, Scott, and asked him to find me a location job that would take me out of LA for a while. He knew the story and was really supportive, so I ended up in the UK for three months doing publicity work for a TV series. I read about their wedding while I was away."

"They didn't want you there when they got married?"

"Oh, yeah. Hank wanted me to be best man, but his agent and the studio bosses wouldn't go for my standing up there with Hank. They didn't even want me there as a guest, so it was just as well I was out of the country. When I got back he was on location in Mexico and Lena had gone with him. It was six months before I saw them again."

"Were things strained between you when you saw them again?"

"Kind of. Hank kept giving me these long looks. I knew what he wanted, but I couldn't give it to him. I couldn't get in the way. Apart from the risk of some scuzzy paparazzi guy getting a photograph of us together, and the fallout that would cause, I just couldn't hurt Lena. She's always been a fragile soul, so easily pushed to the edge. I could tell they were both doing drugs, I just didn't know how bad it was at first.

"Hank would call me, high as a kite. He would cry, tell me he still loved me, wanted me back, railed at everyone for messing up our lives, said he wanted to give everything up, just to have me back again. I was worried Lena would hear him and go to pieces, or someone on their staff would blab. The only person I ever trusted was Sophia, Hank's secretary. She stayed on after Hank's death, really to look after Lena. I don't know if she'll be able to stand Ryan Hart." He sighed and leaned back into the couch cushions. "Sorry, I've been ranting on and on for way too long. Boring you to death probably."

"Hardly boring me," Edward said, sliding his hand over Alex's thigh. "I am really sorry you've been through so much heartache." He moved closer and Alex enclosed him in an embrace. Edward sought Alex's lips and gasped with rapture when Alex opened to him and kissed him with a feverish passion.

When they broke the kiss, Alex said, his voice rasping from lack of breath, "When we first met I asked what troubled you. I know you said you didn't want to *burden* me with it, and now I've been the one to unload on you."

"In comparison to yours, there's nothing very original about my story," Edward told him. "Just another tale of a small town boy disowned by his family for being different, or, in their words, an abomination."

"Oh, Edward." Alex held him as close to his own body as he could, still mindful of Edward's physical pain. "No one could be less of an abomination than you. You are a beautiful man, inside and out, and don't ever let anyone tell you different."

"Thank you." Edward buried his face in the warmth of Alex's neck. "Your opinion of me is all that matters."

"Likewise," Alex whispered. "I think we're through with talking about the past. We have the future to look forward to."

"Yes." Edward closed his eyes and sent up a silent prayer that, somehow, what Alex had just said meant that the future he looked forward to included them both, together.

Chapter Eleven

Two weeks later

Alex gritted his teeth when he passed Scott's office and heard Jeff's rough voice as he railed at Scott about something that was obviously displeasing him. He almost made it to his office without being seen, but Margie, Scott's secretary spotted him on her way back from the coffee machine and hissed at him, "Scott needs you in his office soon as you're here, he said."

Damn. He'd been afraid of that ever since he'd last spoken with Lena. For the past week the TV entertainment news, popular magazines and the tabloid press had been overflowing with an almost breathless expectation waiting for the 'big announcement'. Now it was finally here—the wedding date—after what Alex considered the shortest engagement ever. Well, probably not the shortest ever, but darn close. It amazed Alex that each time they spoke Lena sounded so upbeat about marrying Ryan Hart. Could there be more to the guy than had met Alex's eye on the few occasions he'd been in Hart's company?

Last night Lena had asked him what he'd been dreading. Would he give her away at the forthcoming nuptials?

"Please, Alex, please," she'd begged him, "you're my best friend and the closest one I have to family now."

"Lena..." He'd tried to have her see what effect this would have on Jeff, her agent, and Ryan, her husband-to-be. He knew neither man cared for him simply because of his and Lena's lasting friendship, and, in their minds, his undue influence over her. "You know this won't go down well. How about Ryan's dad? He seems like a nice enough guy." Alex had met Hart's parents at the engagement party.

"Alex!" There was Margie again waving her arms at him as if she were bringing a plane in to land.

He sighed with resignation, then straightening his shoulders, he knocked lightly on the open door to Scott's office. "You wanted to see me, Scott?"

"Uh, yeah, Alex, come on in. Jeff has something he wants to say."

Oh, oh, here it comes. "'Morning, Jeff," he said breezily as he took a seat in front of Scott's desk. "How goes it?"

Lena's agent stared at him as if he was suffering from chronic indigestion. "Alex." He shifted uncomfortably in his seat. "Lena has asked me if I would persuade you to give her away at her wedding to Ryan Hart."

"Oh?" Alex gave him an innocent look. "Have they set the date then?"

"Yes," Jeff said through clenched teeth. "March twentieth. Well?"

"Well, will I give Lena away?" He knew something big must have happened for Jeff to be here asking—no, trying to *persuade* him to give Lena away. He could only guess what it was. For a moment he considered making Jeff sweat more than he already was, then he relented. No point in being as belligerent as the idiot. "Of course I will. It will be an honor—and I thank you, Jeff, for asking on Lena's behalf."

Jeff's face contorted into an expression that was halfway between a sickly smile and a need to go to the bathroom. "Fine," he rasped. "I'll let her know you're on board with it." Without another word, he rose rapidly from his seat and hurried toward the door like his pants were on fire.

"Oh, man..." Scott grinned from ear to ear. "Don't you wish you'd been a fly on the wall earlier?"

"Not really. I think I can guess what he had to say."

"That Lena told him the wedding was off and he was fired if he didn't *persuade* you to give her away?"

Alex smiled wryly. "We spoke last night and she did ask me if I'd give her away. I told her I'd love to but it would cause too many problems, mainly from Jeff, but perhaps her intended also. She ended up saying she'd take care of it, but I didn't think she'd go as far as threatening Jeff with the sack."

"And from Jeff's attitude he was majorly surprised," Scott said. "I guess Lena's not the fragile little butterfly everyone takes her for."

"She can be feisty when people try to get in the way of what she wants," Alex replied, "and she's becoming more and more aware of just how valuable she is in the industry."

"You think this marriage to Hart will work out?"

"I honestly don't know, Scott." Alex sighed and ran a hand through his hair. "I want more than anything for her to be loved and be happy. We've had a lot of conversations about her letting go of Hank's memory just enough so that she could be open to loving someone else. Whether Ryan Hart is the right guy, I don't know, but she seems to like him, and I think she's surprised him on a few occasions. He's a bit of a blowhard, but a couple of times I've seen her call him out on his bullshit and it looked like he was able to laugh it off. Who knows? They just might be able to make it work."

Scott frowned. "Doesn't sound like the romance of the century."

"No, it's not—but it could be what they both need. Only time will tell."

* * * *

Edward let himself into the apartment he shared with Kevin and Troy, feeling very glad it was Friday and he had the weekend off. He'd moved back in a week ago even though Alex had told him he could stay at his house for as long as he liked. While Edward appreciated the offer, Alex hadn't exactly asked him to move in and he still had two months left on the lease, which he felt obligated to honor. They were seeing each other practically every night and Edward frequently stayed over at Alex's place, but he wasn't taking anything for granted. He'd been let down that way before, and to be fair, Alex hadn't said anything about commitment or relationship. The sex was always fantastic, and since Edward was now fully recovered, they had resumed fucking each other. But there had to be more than sex to bond them together...didn't there?

Things were quite a bit easier at the apartment since he and Troy had formed a much better understanding of one another – barring the occasional verbal zinger Troy was so capable of handing out. The other good thing was that his car had been returned to him after being impounded as evidence.

"Anyone home?"

"Just me, Mother."

Troy. His roomie appeared from the kitchen "How're things in the world of high finance?" he asked, grinning.

"Busy. I'm bushed and need a shower." He sniffed the air. "What smells so good?"

"You mean apart from *moi*?" Troy gave him a hug and a perfunctory kiss on the cheek, something he'd been doing regularly since his release from the hospital.

'A whole new Troy.' Edward had kidded him by singing it to the tune from the movie *Aladdin*. He still couldn't quite get over the fact that the two of them had become such good friends.

"I am cooking, believe it or not, dinner for my hunk of a detective who will be here in about an hour or so," Troy said. "You're welcome to join us if you're not doing anything."

Edward chuckled. "I do not think so. Never let it be said I played third wheel. Besides, Alex is taking me to dinner. He says he has a surprise for me."

"Really?" Troy raised an eyebrow. "Another one?"

"What d'you mean?"

Troy gave him a wicked smile. "I should think you get a surprise every time he whips it out of his pants. It's big, isn't it?"

Despite this being an old game Troy loved to play, Edward laughed. "Troy, is nothing sacred? Do I ever ask you about the dimensions of Mark's dick? No, I do not, because I happen to think that such things are private."

"You're no fun, Southern-fried, but I still like you. Anyway, to answer your previous question, what smells so good is the beef stroganoff I'm serving tonight on a table set for two with candlelight and wine."

"Oh, so your invitation to join you was made in the hope I'd say no?"

Troy attempted a shamefaced expression. "Well, if you *really* hadn't anyplace else to go..."

Edward laughed then asked, "Where's Kevin?"

Troy grimaced. "Sourpuss is going home for the weekend, thank fuck. I even got him a cheap ticket at the agency just so he wouldn't change his mind. Hey, by the way..." Troy brightened considerably as he continued. "How could I forget? Mark told me those creeps, Walter and Garth, were sentenced today. He's bringing the paper over, the one it's reported in. It didn't make headlines, because it was only about a couple of gay boys, of course, but Walter got fifteen years and Garth ten."

Edward sighed. "That's a relief. I kept thinking they might just get off with probation or something."

"No way. Mark said they'd get years in jail."

"Well, thank God we can finally put all that behind us." He and Troy smiled at one another then Troy put his arms around Edward and they hugged.

"Yeah," Troy said softly. "Out of all that crap came something worthwhile. You and me got to be real friends..."

"And you got a hunky detective in your life," Edward added.

"Right. Life is good."

Edward had to agree.

* * * *

The restaurant Alex had chosen was one Edward hadn't been to before and from its opulent exterior, he could tell it was going to be very expensive. One of the things Edward had insisted on when he and Alex went out was that they go Dutch. After some argument Alex had given in, but tonight... *Wow,* Edward thought, *this is going to strain the budget.*

"Uh, Alex, this looks a bit extravagant," he said as Alex valet-parked his car.

"Don't worry, you're a guest tonight." He got out of the car and paused to slip on his dark blue blazer.

"But—"

"Just relax and enjoy yourself," Alex whispered. He helped Edward put on his jacket then passed his keys to the valet attendant.

"But we agreed that we go fifty-fifty on dinners," Edward argued as they entered the restaurant's lobby. "Omigod, Alex, this place is—is unbelievable." Now he understood why Alex had said 'wear a jacket'. Everyone was dressed to kill, the ladies in fashionable evening dresses, all the men in suits or sports jackets and slacks, a few even in tuxes. Edward couldn't help gaping. He felt as if he knew some of these people... They looked familiar. Was he hallucinating?

Beside him, stunning as always, Alex greeted a couple who approached them, smiling. "Alex"—the man extended his hand—"good to see you again."

"Likewise." Alex shook the man's hand and received a kiss on the cheek from the tall woman by his side. He turned to Edward and took his hand, drawing him closer. "Keith, Nicole, this is my friend Edward."

Edward's knees almost gave out when Keith Urban shook his hand and gave him a friendly clap on the shoulder. "Nice meeting you," he said in his distinctive New Zealand drawl, while Nicole Kidman gave Edward a pretty smile.

"So, are you here for the big announcement?" Nicole asked.

"Uh..." Edward didn't have a clue what the beautiful star was talking about.

"Yes, we are," Alex said.

"Good, so we'll see you later inside." They drifted off and Alex took Edward's arm and led him over to the lobby bar. "You look like you need a drink."

"I just met Keith Urban and Nicole Kidman, you bet I need a drink. And they acted like you're all friends together — and there's, oh my God, there's Zachary *Quinto*, on his own. I thought he was dating someone..."

Alex laughed. "I thought you weren't interested in celebrities."

"Well, I pay more attention since I met you — but Zachary Quinto is Spock in *Star Trek*. That's huge!"

"What would you like?" Alex asked as the barman hurried toward them.

"Oh, anything."

"How about champagne?"

"Isn't that more for a celebration?"

"This is a celebration. You don't remember? Edward, I'm hurt."

Edward stared at him in a panic. What had he forgotten? A holiday? Alex's birthday? No, he knew that was in May and his own wasn't until September. What then?

"What is it?"

"It's exactly thirty-two days since we met at the Rockin' Bar."

"Oh." He watched as Alex's somber expression morphed into a big smile. "Oh right, that definitely calls for champagne."

Alex ordered two glasses of champagne and they watched quietly as the barman popped the cork and poured the bubbling brew. Alex handed him a glass and touched his lightly to Edward's. "Cheers."

"Cheers." Their eyes met over the tops of their glasses. "Thirty-two days," Edward murmured after his first sip. "Wow, we're like an old married couple already."

Alex raised an eyebrow and Edward cursed mentally. *Shit, why did I say something dumb like that?* "Hey, I forgot to tell you..." He figured a quick change of subject was a good idea right about now. "Troy was making dinner when I got home — for Detective Mark and himself. Candlelight and wine, Troy said. Seems like things are getting serious."

"Yes, it does." Alex chuckled. "I wonder if the good detective knows what he's getting into."

Edward grinned. "I think if anyone can handle Troy, it's Detective McLennan. Troy looks at him like he's a god on earth."

They were interrupted at that moment by a maître d' who asked if they were Mr. Martinez and Mr. Conway.

"That's us," Alex told him, winking at Edward.

"Your table is ready, sirs. Please follow me."

Edward couldn't resist glancing left and right as they were led through the crowded restaurant. Everywhere he looked he recognized faces even if he couldn't put a name to some of them.

A table for two in this place? Alex must have some pull...

However, the table the maître d' conducted them to was not just for them. A large party was already seated. Everyone seemed to know Alex, who introduced Edward to them, but the long list of names was too much to digest all at once, especially as there was so much chatter and 'air kissing' going on. After they were seated Edward noticed there were still two empty seats opposite them.

"Where's the happy couple?" someone asked.

"Heading this way, even as we speak," a man with a sour expression said in reply.

"That's Jeff Harding," Alex whispered, his lips tickling Edward's ear. "Lena's agent. He and I don't get along."

"This may seem like a silly question," Edward whispered back, "but why am I here? I feel like a party crasher or something."

Alex slipped a hand under the table and squeezed Edward's thigh. "You're not. You were invited. Believe me, I wouldn't be here if you hadn't been."

Edward could see the sincerity of that remark in Alex's warm brown eyes and he relaxed enough to cover Alex's hand, still on his thigh, with his own. He heard a ripple of applause behind them. He turned to look and recognized Lena Miles and Ryan Hart as they walked down the center aisle of the restaurant, acknowledging the waves and cries of greeting from the diners. It was like he imagined a royal occasion to be, and in a way it was— Hollywood royalty. Lena was, without a doubt, a beautiful woman. Her statuesque figure, auburn hair that cascaded round her shoulders, and the slight Asian cast to her eyes gave her an exotically different appearance from the usual blonde and bland Hollywood type. Edward was very much in awe when Lena, ignoring everyone else at the table, ran into Alex's open arms and hugged him tightly.

"Thank you," she said, and kissed his cheek. Then she turned and smiled. "You must be Edward. I'm Lena and this is my fiancé Ryan."

Edward's hand was taken in an over-the-top hearty handshake by the handsome movie star. "Glad you could make it, Alex... Edward." He turned his attention to the woman who had been sitting next to Edward. "Hi, Mom..."

Lena finally waved to everyone else at the table then she and Ryan took their seats. Waiters descended on them, champagne bottles at the ready, and the man Alex had called Jeff Harding stood and proposed a toast to the 'happy couple'.

As soon as he'd finished, Lena piped up, "And I want to thank my best friend Alex for agreeing to give me away and making my wedding day complete." She blew Alex a kiss and everyone applauded, except her agent, and Edward couldn't help but notice that Ryan Hart's enthusiasm was half-hearted at best.

Alex grinned at him. "Do I have lipstick on my face?"

"Just a smidge." Edward chuckled. "So, I'm guessing that you giving Lena away isn't popular with everyone—including the groom?"

Alex sighed. "Yeah, my being buddies with Lena is a sore point with Jeff and Hart. Once they're married it'll settle down. There are already plans for Lena and him to do some big epic together. Most of the filming will be done in New Zealand so it'll give them time to really get to know one another."

Edward nodded, but he couldn't help thinking that perhaps 'getting to know one another' should come before the marriage.

The rest of the evening went by in a welter of champagne, too much food and a constant stream of well-heeled men and women coming by the table to wish Lena and Ryan all happiness. Sitting opposite Lena, Edward could tell she was over it, while Ryan Hart appeared to be lapping up the attention. At one point Edward and Lena's eyes met and he gave her a sympathetic look, which she acknowledged with a little smile.

"Ready to go?" Alex must have been reading his mind.

"Whenever you are."

"That would be now." Alex stood, and, taking Edward's hand, he led him to the other side of the table to say goodnight to Lena.

She looked up at him and managed a tired smile. "The wedding rehearsal's on the nineteenth, darling," she told Alex. "And bring Edward, too." After hugs and goodnights from Lena and several others at the table, they made their way to the exit.

The cool evening air outside as they waited for the parking valet to bring Alex's car was a relief from the crowded and noisy restaurant.

"So, what d'you think?" Alex asked.

"Lena's lovely," Edward replied, "and underneath that fragile façade I got a hint of quite a determined woman."

"Very observant of you. You think you could get used to this kind of shindig?"

"Once in a while would be all right. I don't know if I could handle that kind of crowd every night. Why d'you ask?"

Their car arrived in front of them and Alex waited until they'd climbed in and he'd pulled away from the restaurant before continuing. "Well, I was thinking that since I introduced you to some of my clients and associates tonight, they'll be expecting to see you with me the next time I'm invited to dinner or some kind of function. In fact, eventually I expect to see your name attached to the invitation."

Edward glanced at Alex's profile to see if he was joking. "Are you serious?"

"Very serious. In fact—but damn, I'm not going to ask you while we're in this car."

"Ask me what?"

"You'll have to wait 'til we get to my place."

"But that's a good twenty minutes' drive. C'mon, Alex..." He leaned over and nuzzled Alex's neck. "Tell me what it is you're going to ask me. If it's sex, you know you don't have to ask."

"It's not sex. Well, yes, it is that too, but there's something else, and I want us to be face to face when I ask."

"I could sit on your lap."

Alex laughed. "I want to get us home in one piece, or two pieces, really. Can you wait? I'll go as fast as I can."

"But don't get stopped by a cop. That would just add to the torment of waiting."

* * * *

The moment they were inside Alex's house, he grabbed Edward and held him in a hard embrace. He peppered Edward's face with soft, teasing kisses before taking Edward's lips with an intensity that stole Edward's breath from his body. Edward wrapped his arms round Alex's neck and kissed him back with a fervor to match Alex's. Alex's kisses were always thrilling. The man could do things with his tongue that Edward had never thought he would ever experience. And yet this was even more awesome, and if Edward had his way it would never end.

Alex jerked his head back suddenly and stared into Edward's eyes. The look was compelling and Edward shivered with anticipation. "What?" he whispered.

"Do you love me, Edward?"

They were still so close, their mouths only centimeters apart. Alex's warm breath fanned Edward's lips and drew him in, seeking another kiss.

"Of course I love you," Edward said before closing that tiny, tantalizing gap and tasting Alex's lips again.

Alex tightened his arms around Edward and the kiss they shared completely overwhelmed Edward's senses. A soft, warm moistness stole into his mouth as Alex's tongue once again slid between Edward's parted lips, caressing the inside of his mouth and setting every nerve ending in his body on fire. A long, low moan of complete desire and surrender escaped from his throat.

Alex leaned back a little, and again those deep brown eyes were fixed on Edward's. "I love you too, Edward. Thirty-two—no, make that thirty-three days as of midnight—isn't a long time, but it's long enough for me to know I'd like you to move in with me and share my life. Will you, Edward?"

When Edward didn't answer, Alex continued, "I know tonight was crazy and maybe a little hard to deal with, but it's just a part of my job. Lena's my friend but she's also a client of Scott's agency…"

Edward put a finger over Alex's lips. "Yes," he said. "Yes, I will move in with you and share your life. There is nothing I want more than that. I want to be with you—craziness and all."

"I just wanted you to see what you might have to put up with—not every night, of course, and you can pick and choose which shindigs you want to go to."

"Alex, it's okay. Just being with you is enough. All I'll ever need…is you."

Alex held him tighter. "So you'll move in right away?"

"Well, I have a couple more months on the lease—and I don't want to leave the guys in the lurch."

"Right, but you can stay here too?"

"You know," Edward gave him a quick kiss on the lips, "I know of a much better place to have this conversation."

Alex nuzzled Edward's neck. "And where would that be?"

"One guess."

Instead of answering, Alex picked him up and charged into the bedroom where he flung Edward onto the bed then jumped on top of him.

"You know what?" he growled into Edward's ear.

"What?" Edward squirmed under him, tugging at Alex's shirt.

"I think we're done talking."

Edward sighed. "Good, I've always heard it's rude to talk with your mouth full."

About the Author

J.P Bowie was born in Scotland and toured British theatres in numerous musical shows including Stephen Sondheim's Company.

Emigrated to the States and worked in Las Vegas, Nevada for the magicians Siegfried and Roy as their Head of Wardrobe at the Mirage Hotel. Currently living in Henderson, Nevada.

J.P Bowie loves to hear from readers. You can find his contact information, website details and author profile page at http://www.totallybound.com.

Totally Bound Publishing